"STARCLASH proves once again that Ron Collins is a master of the science fiction adventure story—not the crazy stuff you remember from the pulps, but the kind of interstellar adventure that has believable characters, plotting that makes sense, and a future that rings true."

Mike Resnick
Hugo Award–winning author of *Kirinyaga*

STARCLASH

STEALING THE SUN
BOOK 4

RON COLLINS

SKYFOX
PUBLISHING
Science Fiction

For Mom and Dad, who've always helped me reach for the stars.

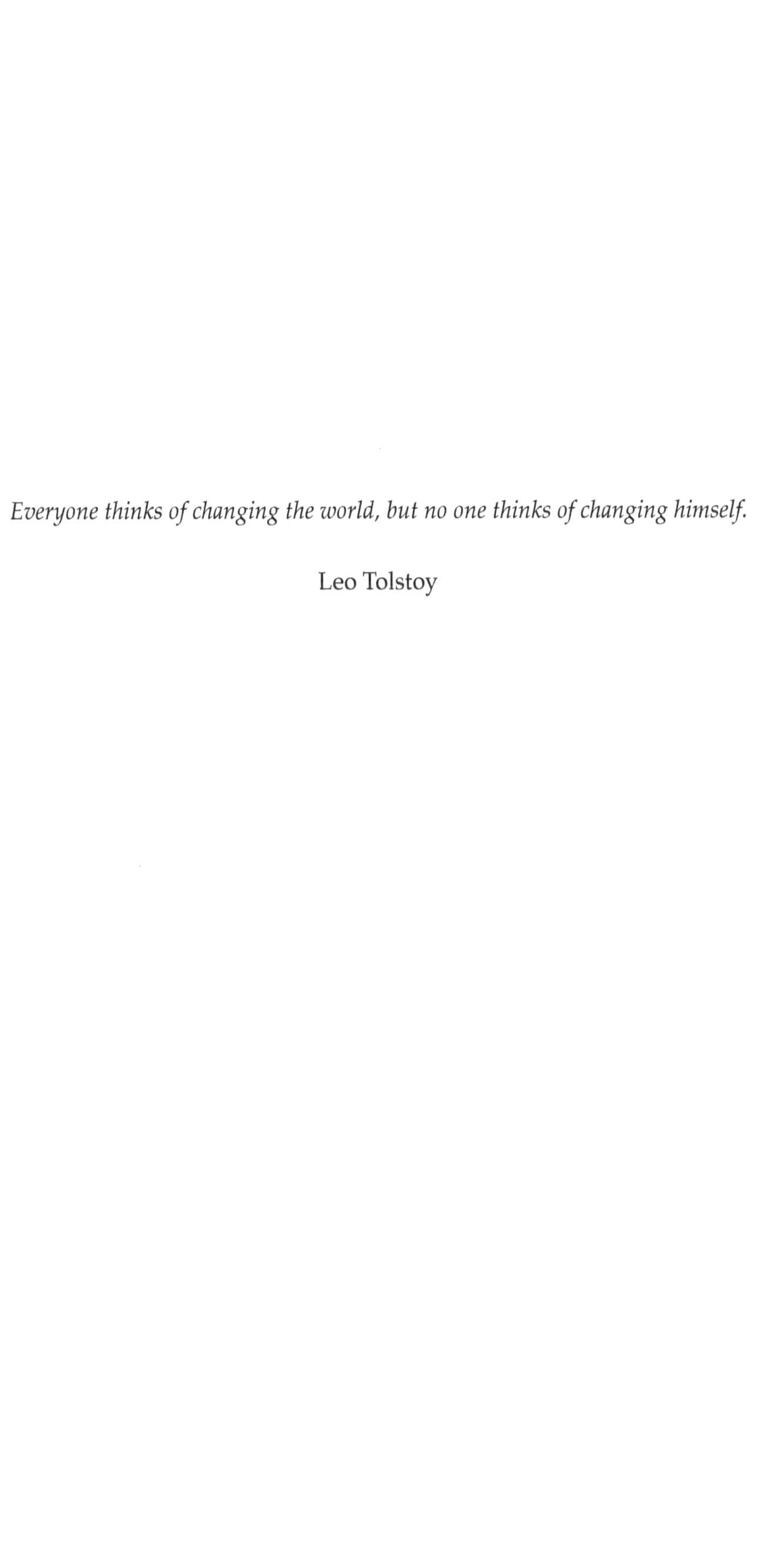

Everyone thinks of changing the world, but no one thinks of changing himself.

Leo Tolstoy

INTRODUCTION

It seems to me that we in the United States are entering a period where we're once again asking ourselves what is, for us, a question we come around to again and again—that being: Who are we?

The options are several.

Are we a kind and giving society?

Are we a nurturing community?

Are we a selfish "I got mine" people?

Are we a capitalistic, driven machine that lets markets decide our fates?

Are we the proverbial melting pot of communities that somehow finds a way to make it all work despite our clear and present differences?

Do we give more than we take, take more than we give, or take only what we give?

Are we the lone ranger—the ruggedly individualistic cowboy who rides out of town to find his own way, and suffers the fate of being posse bait if he goes too far?

Which brings me to the question that feeds this story.

It's complex, right?

Complicated.

Confusing.

And for some, me included, the question that keeps coming back into my mind is the push that has driven through this particular story.

What can I do?

What should I do?

The world is so big, right? How much can I change? How much does my voice count? How much does a vote count?

Yes, just how much energy should I spend dealing with some of the events of the day?

In the end, I decided that what I was really dealing with was a much more basic question. How much can one person matter? How much change can one person create by their decisions?

Technically, I suppose all stories have a bit of this question in them, but that was what I was asking myself as I brought these characters together again. That's what I was wondering.

In the end, I'm still not sure I have the answer.

I suspect that the answer is different for each person—because life is like that, mostly. There are so few simple situations. So few binary settings. So I suspect that the amount of change you or I can each make is variable.

In the end, though, unless we actually choose to do something, the answer is "none." Do nothing, create no change.

But take an action, and then change is possible.

Which brings us back to the beginning.

To take an action that drives change, it seems to me that we (meaning you or I or anyone else, specifically including the characters in this little story of mine) need to answer that most basic question for ourselves.

Who are we?

What kind of world do we want to live in?

Then, of course, we get to the harder question.

What are we willing to sacrifice to get there?

Ron Collins
December 2016

PROLOGUES

SUMMER

During the summer months of Torrance Black's eighth year, his father often stood with a pair of binoculars in the field behind their backyard, looking up at the night sky. The Wisconsin breeze would be thick with the smells of timothy grass. Katydids and crickets would sing. Meanwhile, his dad would point out the dippers, and Draco, Cepheus, and the North Star—all circumpolar in the northern sky. He would show Torrance Cygnus, Sagittarius, and Hercules, and tell him how Scorpius was running across the horizon chasing Orion, who would be hiding on the other side of the world until November came.

Other kids remembered the dippers, the big one in particular. But Torrance always considered Cassiopeia to be his favorite constellation because its W-shaped scatter floated in the sky like a huge wing and because he knew it ran along the Milky Way. His father once told him Cassiopeia's story—how she connived to keep Perseus and Andromeda from marrying, and how Jupiter hung her upside down in the northern sky to atone for her sins.

Later in his life, Torrance would spend considerably more time learning legends about Cassiopeia and the rest of the constellations as told from different cultures. These stories did nothing but increase his love of the sky as a whole, and as he grew older and dealt with difficult times he found himself going to the night sky and remembering those nights with his dad. Thinking about the people throughout history who had gazed up at these very same stars and seen the very same things he was looking at right then always made him feel better.

Eta Cass was a bright dot on the lower leg of the W.

It became his favorite star on the day he learned that, despite being a single dot in his field glasses, it was really a binary pair, a G spectrum star that orbited with a K spectrum star at a period of just under five hundred standard years.

Knowing things like this made him feel more than smart. There was something ancient, powerful about knowing this single dot in the sky that oscillated colors between gold, red, yellow, and purple was really two stars.

Torrance learned several things that summer when he was eight.

He learned his father could speak volumes with a single grunt. He learned that spiders built their webs at night, and that it's a good idea to wave a stick along your path as you walk through the gloom. But mostly, he learned that when unanswered questions were gnawing at the pit of his stomach, discovering the truth—finding out how things really were—filled that ache in a more satisfying way than he could possibly describe.

TWO STANDARDS AGO

U3 Ship *Icarus*
   Atropos Orbit, Eta Cassiopeia System
   Local Date: Conejo 12, 7
   Local Time: 0720

The support rail was cold against Deidra Francis's palms. The observation panel ahead of her opened to a star-patterned view of deep space. Below her, rows of command stations fell away in rings that made her perch at the top of the command bridge feel like being on the balcony of a theater.

The crew prepared for jump.

They were a calm group, the definition of professional, which made her feel even worse about her own anxiety. They moved with simple precision and spoke with hushed tones that the ship's noise reduction system muted even further. Air from the ventilation system was cool and dry.

A nervous tick played across the corner of Deidra's lips.

The mission profile would take them to the Solar System—back to Miranda Station—for the first time since Universe Three's brilliantly devised raid had derailed the United Government's Star Drive program, first by destroying *Sunchaser* and stealing *Icarus* and *Einstein*, then by returning with *Icarus* to destroy Miranda's production facilities. She had still been a girl then, barely thirteen. She was nearly nineteen now. If everything went right today, their mission would do considerably more damage to UG's situation than even that success had managed.

It was only a week before that U3 had been informed Professor Jorge Catazara, the driving intellect behind the UG's thrust to expand Star Drive technology, had finally grown so disenchanted with his government's policies that he could see what damage he was doing. Today Universe Three was going to help him change sides.

They had extracted people before, of course.

So often, in fact, that most of the Universe Three citizens were already in the Eta Cass system and several other sympathizers had been recovered, too—all in ops designed just like this one, jump to a spot in space, pick up a rider, and hop the hell out of the zone before things got too hairy. They had done it often enough that the tactic was now more than a thorn in the UG's side. So often that even UG's own journalists were asking pointed questions like: *How can the UG be winning the war if Universe Three is so free to operate?*

UG politicians were still trying to get away with answering these questions with their standard talking points, saying that this wasn't really a war so much as a continuation of the skirmishes that had been so prevalent before the Operation Starburst catastrophe. But Katriana Martinez, Deidra's mentor, was still attached to Universe Three's security teams and Deidre knew Katriana well enough by now to be able to read her. Even her mentor's silences told Deidra the answer was growing threadbare among UG citizens.

That anyone bought those arguments in the first place stood testimony to her father's view that most people preferred comfortable lies to painful truths.

Universe Three had never gone after someone like Catazara, though.

This kind of defection would be hard to ignore.

Everything had to happen just so.

The op had to be perfect.

"Is everything progressing?" Captain Keyes said as he came from his briefing room to stand beside her.

Matt Anderson and the rest of his three-member security detail were still in the compartment, gathering up material in preparation of the jump and launch.

Deidra stood straighter.

She had been the one managing preparations, but this was still the captain's ship.

For now, anyway.

"Yes, Captain," she said. "Prelim testing is complete. Impulse power is functional for our arrival on station, trim bursts too, in case we need fine tuning. The crew is accounted for, and the skimmers are all on full power and full green status. We're cross-indexing our navigation calibrations now. Once those are finished, we'll be ready for your command. Should be any moment."

It was standard protocol that whenever either *Icarus* or *Einstein* jumped, the target parameters would be run through both ships' navigation simulators to ensure they were appropriate. *"Two sets of eyes,"* Katriana Martinez had told her back in the earliest days. *"You want it to be right."*

Deidra had argued about the idea of redundant passes, preferring to move more quickly, until Katriana pulled out the big guns.

"Nothing the UG does works right the first time, Deidra," she had said. *"Do you want to be like them?"*

That phrase had been enough to change her mind all by itself, but later she remembered Ellyn Parker's catchphrase: *Make sure you're right, then go ahead.* She had never again complained about the idea of taking pains to do something right.

"Thank you, Director," Keyes said.

"My father is the director," she replied.

The captain's eyes sparkled as his lips tightened into a gentle smile.

"Perhaps I was speaking in future tense."

"Flattery will get you everywhere, is it?"

"Only if it turns out to be right."

Matt Anderson stepped out of the room, followed by his team. He had grown more angular over the years, and now filled out his mission jacket in ways that would be attractive to a certain type of woman—of which Deidra most certainly was not.

Even if she was, she couldn't ever see being with him.

With the names *Francis* and *Anderson*, the two shared the baggage of having expectation heaped upon them. They had been on the fast path together, each quickly taking more responsibility than their ages might have suggested was intelligent. Matt, now twenty-five, was ruggedly cut and boyishly handsome. Deidra was seen as bright and judgmental. She understood how people matched them up in their minds—the storybook romance and all. But it wasn't happening. Matt's demeanor made her anxious. She didn't like his disregard for the command, or, to put it better, she didn't like how he only had respect for the command when the command agreed with his viewpoints or when it was in his own best interest. Beyond that, it was obvious Matt Anderson didn't like the fact that she was quicker than he was, and she could tell he held discomfort that *her* father was the leader of Universe Three, and that *his* father was second in command.

None of that was her fault, of course.

All that mattered is that, despite the fact that both of them had been given leadership roles on this mission—Deidra coordinating the ship's prejump activities and Matt leading the rendezvous flight—the pairing of Matt Anderson and Deidra Francis was not going to happen.

"We're on our way now, Captain," Matt said as he led his team out of the briefing room. "The mission team will be on station in three minutes."

"Thank you, Mr. Anderson," Keyes said.

Deidra glanced at the captain, then turned her gaze to the forward observation panels where prejump data scrolled by.

"I notice you didn't call him Director."

The captain squared himself and took in a raspy breath through his nose.

"No," he said. "I didn't, did I?"

———

The jump to superluminal occurred exactly on time.

Having seen the light show before, and given that Uranus was surrounded by buckets of space junk that made being perfect even more important than usual, Deidra focused on the ship's position readings throughout the maneuver.

Their "splashdown" was within a hundred meters of her projection.

"Nice work," Captain Keyes said.

She chuffed under her breath. That level of accuracy was almost unheard of. The hundreds of test jumps she had simulated were proving their value. She couldn't wait to get back to Katriana to share their success.

"Thank you, sir," she replied through her smile.

Their splashdown point was designed to put Miranda, one of Uranus's moons, between them and the UG space station, a position that would protect them from detection for at least a few minutes.

By the time she checked the numbers a second time, Anderson's team had already jettisoned in the pair of Z-pad skimmers.

———

With the planet looming behind them, Matt Anderson guided the Z-pad toward Miranda's "western" horizon—though the fact that Miranda's orbit around Uranus was ninety degrees off the ecliptic made that call relative.

"Running on silent from here out," Tamira Weston said into the radio from the left-hand seat.

"Roger," came the reply.

Anderson was dialed in now, heart racing despite all the training sims. The cockpit space pressed in on him. Colors from the control panel seemed more vivid than they ever had before. He heard Weston speak, but only registered it because they had run this mission a couple hundred times in the simulator and the tone of her voice was now ingrained in the process.

They approached the dark side of Miranda and hugged the terrain.

Its surface caught enough reflection from Uranus to show that

Miranda was craggy and lined, gouged and pitted with layers of impact craters that marked its age.

"Looks like some kind of melted crystal," Westin said as the Z-pads winged over its surface.

Anderson grunted.

He had seen pictures.

No need to waste brain waves.

Miranda had no atmosphere. Its surface was mostly ice, which was something the United Government considered an advantage when they first decided to put so much of their Star Drive manufacturing capability here—the self-contained supply of water meant vast amounts of freely available hydrogen, which made for easy processing of rocket fuel and greater flexibility in their ability to create material at the atomic level.

Using Miranda as a blind, Anderson's flight plan called for them to avoid detection by hugging the ground, then fly a burst straight up to the station, approaching the target from below like a balloon buster from the earliest days of air combat. Anderson's unit would cover the approach while Shay Kai's unit would set down to pick up the package. He had wanted to be the one to take the set-down role, but his father was adamant—a mission like this was no time for nepotism, and Kai was the better flyer.

They were on half power to reduce the profile of their emissions when they crested the "edge of darkness," or point of no return where detection was possible.

The Z-pads passed that point.

The station loomed as a bright point in the blackness of space.

The guidance panel suddenly lit up like a city street, and the threat detection system went to full jam mode.

It was too early for that.

Damn it.

If their intel was right, the pair now had something in the range of two minutes before the UG security systems would flag them as actual threats rather than merely unknown foreign material.

A blue light flared on the station.

Anderson's threat computer blared.

So much for freaking intel.

"Dive left, and begin your direct approach now," he called, breaking silence as his heart rate spiked. "Full engines."

His throat was suddenly dry.

He turned the Z-pad left, then right. Then he pointed straight at the station, putting the craft nearly on its ass end, and hit full power.

The back of his seat felt like it was going to come out his breastbone.

The station got big.

Kai's Z-pad took a similar juke.

A beam of light flashed past them.

Plasma blast.

Shit.

Goddamned double shit.

They were not supposed to have a plasma cannon in place.

"Split and run," he called out.

Kai's skimmer peeled off first, Anderson's a moment later despite the fact that he was the one giving the order. The second plasma blast almost took his right-side pod off, but somehow he avoided it.

Westin said something he didn't catch.

He jammed the joystick right, and brought the Z-pad into a proper cover path. "Ready guns," he said to her.

"Already done," she replied in a way that told him what she had just said.

Westin was the communications specialist on the mission, but she had cross-trained on the weapon systems, and was solid with them. That was the U3 way—cross-pollination, multiple skills to ensure operations can withstand loss.

As the station came nearer she sprayed a blast from the laser system out in front of them, catching the plasma cannon in one blast. Their fire probably wouldn't totally kill it, but if the atmospheric seals on the cannon's pod were breached it could give them thirty seconds or more before the weapon could be used again…which would at least get them into place.

Kai formed up beside them.

Miranda Station grew huge.

Just as they had done in the sim, Kai broke off and looped around to an emergency platform just outside the primary landing bay. Anderson brought his Z-pad to a course that followed a seam in that same bay, and Westin laid down another line of laser fire that melted down the bay doors.

If that worked, at least they wouldn't have company for a while.

He hit trim boosters and pulled severe g's on the double-back.

Westin screamed to keep the blood in her head, which reminded him to do that, too.

The return path gave Westin a second shot at disabling the bay doors, which she took. An orange flare came from the emergency pad. The passenger in Kai's craft carried a handheld laser, just as Westin did in case they would have to substitute. They were shooting at something.

Anderson couldn't see what happened, but Kai's Z-pad lifted off, and Anderson took that as the sign that the package was on board.

"Ready to run," Kai's voice came over the radio in a calm monotone.

The shortest path between two points is a straight line, and this time there was no subtlety to their flight path. The two of them headed directly for Miranda's horizon.

"Hit that cannon again!" Anderson screamed.

Westin was already shooting.

The escape run was probably the longest minute and a half of his life.

"Professor on board," Kai reported when they crossed over the edge of darkness and back to Miranda's backside.

"Outstanding," Anderson said, breathing properly again.

He pulled his hand off the joystick, and flexed a cramp away.

"Good flying," Westin said.

"Thanks," he replied.

It was hours later before he realized he hadn't commented on her shooting.

———

Deidra brushed the palms of her hands over her hips as she stood in the docking bay control room.

The two Z-pads set down.

Her first reaction was relief that both had returned. Her second was to think about everything she had to do.

"Close the bay door, Abke," the controller said.

The doors ground closed.

After the vacuum was filled, Deidra stepped through the double locks to stand beside the skimmer.

This was easy, she thought, as she waited for the professor. Like fish in a barrel. At this rate Universe Three would be able to control their own fate in no time.

The door popped open.

A disheveled man stepped out.

He was about her height. Thin enough that his clothes hung off him like drapes. His skin was light brown. His face hollowed at the cheeks. His hair was dark and stereotypically unkempt.

"Welcome aboard *Icarus*, Professor Catazara," Deidra said as she offered her hand, "and welcome to Universe Three."

ONE STANDARD AGO

Atropos, Eta Cassiopeia System
    Local Date: Kalnas 19, 8
    Local Time: 1145

Todias Nimchura, a man whose call sign had once been "Yuletide,"
and who had once been the wingman of Alex "Deuce" Jarboe, poured
concrete into its frame. When the material was settled, he used a
spreader to smooth its surface and a smaller trowel to do the detail
work. It was summertime in Atropos City. The heat of Eta Cass, now
risen to its noon-point, beat through the cloth he had tied around his
head and through the sweat-stained shirt he wore over his shoulders.
He smelled of human brine and the coarse grit that coated his face. His
body, already hardened by his military background, had been scoured
and roughened in these past few years, his skin baked to a deeper
brown, his muscles leaned out by a barebones diet of unprocessed
foods and hardened further by backbreaking work.

When the concrete was smooth, he stood, stretched his back, and
squinted up at Eta Cass.

"You waiting for rain or something?"

It was his shift leader, a woman who was no stranger to either sarcasm or biting commentary.

"Just stretching," Nimchura replied.

"Take all the time you need," she said. "Your day's not over 'til the whole thing's poured no matter what you do."

"Yes, ma'am, I get that."

"That'll be the day."

For a moment he thought she was going to sit down and just make his afternoon hell, but she left him alone, heading to the other corner of the plot to harass Gif Johnson.

Nimchura smirked at that.

Johnson was U3 clear through. Had come from a station at Io, where he did the same thing he was doing now—constructing shitty buildings so folks who ran things could have nice places to live. Only difference was that those earlier buildings were all built down under the surface or inside atmospheric domes rather than out here under the open sky.

So Nimchura's smirk was for U3, Gif Johnson, and the entire concept of freedom.

U3 was supposed to be all about freedom, after all.

Freedom this, and freedom that.

As far as Nimchura was concerned, it was all just so much bullshit —no more or no less bullshit than he ever saw out of the United Government, anyway, which was a group who claimed it was all about safety and security but who didn't keep anyone safe or secure unless they could afford it.

That was his thing now—comparing the freedoms he once held with those he had now.

Nearly seven local years had passed since he had been captured, three since he had been given full "freedom" to live among the U3 as a citizen.

As far as he was concerned, it was all the same.

He glanced over his concrete pour and saw it was good.

Concrete was expensive, or at least it was hard to make here on Atropos because they only had a few pieces of the equipment they needed to make small rocks out of big ones. That meant Universe

Three's architects reserved it for foundation work, leaving the rest of their buildings to be made of mudbrick or lumber. The plot he was working on was a set of nine blocks, a meter and a half each side—small enough to avoid settling cracks, large enough to cover reasonable floor space. When this group was poured, he would move to the next, and then the next. Then the rest of the building would be assembled.

This one was going to be a big one—maybe fifty meters to a side. When the building was completed it would be used to make more space-faring equipment.

That was the rumor, anyway.

The scuttlebutt said U3 was going to make another Star Drive ship. They said U3 had studied *Icarus* and *Einstein*. That they were building prototypes and reengineering parts they didn't understand.

Nimchura knew for a fact that U3 had brought scientists and engineers into the project by convincing them to go turncoat. He supposed he should be pissed at that, but after all this time he couldn't manage to bring up any kind of healthy rage about it.

Universe Three's plan was to make one Star Drive ship just to prove they could, then, using buildings with the foundations Todias Nimchura was helping to pour, make more.

That was the rumor, anyway.

And he admitted the rumor made his palms itch.

With his background, Nimchura would probably never be trusted to do much beyond foundation work, and in truth he should probably feel lucky to have that. But Todias Nimchura had once flown XB-25 Firebrands for the United Government Interstellar Command. He dreamed of flying again. The idea was all that kept him going at times. He couldn't imagine ever being happy with a life that consisted of pouring foundations.

He took a deep sigh and bent down to retrieve the canteen he had left in the shade.

The water was lukewarm.

The sounds of other workers filled space around him.

Animals plodding, masons and carpenters calling to each other, pounding on other buildings around him. Every day was the same. The clatter was a dull din that seeped from everywhere at once.

Freedom was a farce, he thought.

He would never fly again.

Nimchura took another swig from the canteen, then put it back in the shade. If he wanted to get home before dark, it was time to get back to work.

THE OLIVE BRANCH

CHAPTER 1

Aldrin Station
Local Date: January 19, 2215
Local Time: 1225

"All it takes to accomplish anything is a single person, properly motivated. This is true of the greatest destructions, and it is true of the most miraculous achievements. One person is all it takes. One person can change everything."

Those words, delivered by an Interstellar Command chaplain, were echoing in Lieutenant Commander Torrance Black's head as the door clicked shut behind him. Finally alone, he let his façade down, removing his hat, leaning back against the hard door, and rubbing his bleary eyes in an attempt to get rid of his headache.

His bay wasn't large for a station like Aldrin, maybe ten meters to a side, but after nearly fifteen locals on *Everguard*, the place felt like a palatial mansion. The walls were white with a thin line of navy piping that marked off the lower third of their height. A sink and shower stall were to the left of the doorway, a closet to his right. The modernistic bed opposite him was a sleek thing with a rounded headboard lined with adjustable reading lights. A work desk filled another corner. Fresh air circulated with a hint of what might have been a waterfall but was probably just mint. The flavor gave the room an edge that was as sharp as the white of the walls.

The morning's ceremony had been a long one, but at least it had been his last. There was nothing else on the public calendar. No events, no meet and greets, no interviews. Just a debrief tomorrow afternoon and this evening's one-on-one meeting with Admiral Umaro.

Both of those should be easy conversations. Simple formalities.

Then his life in the service would be over.

Decommission: the only way to cut bait.

Despite the fact that it was only just past lunch, he was drained now, numb from the unrelenting blur of interrogations, press functions, funerals, and memorials that had unfolded in the aftermath of *Everguard*'s sabotage. He hadn't slept right for weeks, and his body was still healing itself from the wounds he had taken during the attack. The scuttling ceremony alone had nearly killed him.

He slid his hat into a cubby beside the door and let the room's silence surround him. For the first time since arriving on Aldrin, Torrance had an entire afternoon to himself.

Torrance pulled the data cube from his pocket and rolled it between his fingers. Its hardened corners pressed into his skin.

He held it up to the light, thinking about the chaplain's words, which were a not-so-thinly-veiled editorial wherein spirituality, politics, and the human need for revenge had been mixed in such measure as it was impossible to pull them apart.

She had been talking about a warrant officer who had given his life extracting families from the same fires on Rearward deck that had disfigured Marisa Harthing. But the chaplain had also been speaking of one Casmir Francis, the leader of Universe Three, the terrorists who had undertaken this attack.

The crystal was a translucent light blue.

The data inside was from Alpha Beta, or as it was commonly known, Eden, the second planet in the Alpha Centauri A system.

Thomas Kitchell had given the crystal to him the night before the attack. It held copies of files that Government Security Officer Casey had banned Torrance from accessing—files that Torrance was still convinced held proof of an alien life-form.

No one would believe him, though.

Despite astrobiologists having spent literally centuries working to find fully developed intelligence, his experience on *Everguard* made it clear that no one would take his ideas seriously until he coaxed the truth from the data.

If even then.

It didn't help that these same scientists had already moved on, already discounted the Alpha Centauri A system as a possible source of intelligent life. Humanity had identified thousands of planets orbiting thousands of stars, all of which carried organic markers of life —but no one had found clear signs of intelligence. Eden had been studied years ago, and summarily tossed aside.

This is why the loss of the three Star Drive spacecraft and the attack on Miranda Station, which had been the United Government's primary production facility for new Star Drive systems, put a rock the size of an asteroid into his gut. With only *Orion* in service, it was likely to be years before they could mount a serious program to visit these stars. Without those studies, without hands-on experience, Torrance didn't think anyone would ever really buy the idea of intelligent life outside the Solar System. He had his files now, though, and he had financial resources built up over fifteen years of compound interest. So he had time.

He cleared his throat as he shrugged off his dress jacket and laid it carefully across the bed.

The room came outfitted with a more advanced computer system than he had seen before. It used three small projector pods installed near the ceiling, each swiveling to create images and patterns that could be displayed on any surface or as a hologram at any location around the room.

Torrance went to the desk and slid the cube into an interface slot.

The system gave a purple flare as it read the data.

"Let me see the file list please, Abke," he said to the controller. "Please project it to the desk," he said when he realized his command hadn't been completed.

He felt obsolete.

At least *Abke* still stood for Autonomic Bioprocessing Knowledge Engine. The central control system had been installed in every Interstellar Command ship since the years when Interstellar Command had been known as Solar Command.

He wondered if Abke had any idea there was talk of replacing her with a more advanced QE communicator that was still under development. The new system used quantum entanglement, and had the advantage of allowing immediate conversation across interstellar distances. Of course, it came with the disadvantage of being point-to-point rather than broadcast. Two of these new QE comm systems could be linked, but once it was created that link could never be changed. In this way, QE communicators were like those silly "phones" made of paper cups and strings that he made in grade school.

Torrance was pretty sure QE would never fully replace Abke, but he was also pretty sure that government security officers throughout the system would be wetting their pants to get hold of one.

Abke delivered the file list.

Torrance sat at the desk chair, leaned back, and scanned the response.

It was a collection of nearly a thousand files.

The first fifty-five held raw data from every sensor *Everguard* had. Then came the models he and Kitchell had created over the years, and then the scrolling columns of test runs. The names of these records gave him a nostalgic sense of warmth. Each of them represented hours of work. Kitchell had done most of them, too—more than half were date-stamped after Casey had removed Torrance's access. The idea that the kid was actually more interested in the data than Torrance was tore his heart up.

Kitchell deserved better than to get shot up like he had.

As far as Torrance knew, the kid would be going into the Academy when he healed up. That had been the plan, anyway, and Torrance had made it a point to reiterate his recommendation everywhere he went these past three weeks.

At twenty-two, Kitchell had a helluva lot going for him.

Torrance hoped he would find a way to stay in touch.

"Please open and play file Black One," he said.

It was one of his own custom files. One he had created in the earliest days.

Abke played the file.

The room popped and fuzzed with a strange, chaotic rhythm. To most people it would have sounded like simple white noise, but to Torrance it was music. Not structured like human music, but still it worked for him. Something to it gave him comfort, a rhythm or a flow that struck him someplace deep inside. It had been locals since he had last heard it.

As it played on, Torrance bent to review another data file.

Then another.

The music looped around as he scanned more.

Looking at the files gave him an awkward sensation that reminded him of attending a college reunion.

He remembered most of them, but he remembered them differently—he recalled partials here or there, and as he took in each of the files they brought up fragments of ideas that seemed familiar in the same way an old summer vacation spot felt familiar. He recalled that at one time he had considered adjusting the spectral density of the radio wave contact image, but couldn't recall exactly how he had planned to do it—something about boosting frequency distributions in sequential patterns and then building a new language model around the output. But that wasn't quite right.

Somewhere in the mix of his thoughts, an ensign delivered a lunch plate.

He ate it, but afterward he only knew he had done so because of the plate of crumbs he left behind and because by late afternoon he wasn't feeling that pit of hunger he would have gotten if he missed a meal.

He wondered what kind of sandwich it had been.

It wasn't until his alarm rang nearly seven hours later that Torrance realized he was going to be late for his meeting with the admiral.

CHAPTER 2

Atropos, Eta Cassiopeia System
Local Date: Studna 23, 9
Local Time: 0524

Casmir Francis's body merged with the thunderhoof's movements.

The beast's hooves pounded against bare rock. Its breathing rasped to the beat of a steam wheel. Its muscles were cords of steel against Casmir's thighs. He had taken his meds and done his routines. Now he was exercising in what had become his favorite way —riding Thunderbolt, the herd animal he had bonded most closely with.

He felt healthier here than he had ever felt before.

Not cured, of course. Cystic fibrosis doesn't work that way.

Perhaps it was something inherent in the planet. Maybe the food they were growing, or microbes in the air. Or maybe it was just that for the first time in over a decade he was able to follow a routine that allowed him to exercise and take care of himself like Yvonne and Dr.

Iwal wanted him to. Whatever the reason, he was stronger here on Atropos, and as he worked with the thunderhoof to race across the land he felt like he was one with the morning.

The sky over the horizon was that endless shade of purple that happened just before sunrise, especially this time of year. It was Studna, Atropos's version of springtime, that time of year when temperatures were rising and the water would come down in sheets. When it came, anyway. Storms on Atropos were sporadic, but could be serious things.

Studna was an old Czech name for *water well*, though.

Fitting, he supposed, though the calendar's months had not been named for any seasonal aspect. Rather, a set of school kids had mapped and named new constellations as seen from their home. Each month was then named for a constellation but in a different language from Earth. That last made him happy. A calendar should have a sense of wonder to it, and a sense of history. This one did. It was the 23rd of Studna. In three days the month would change to Conejo as Atropos moved through the Rabbit and into the true spring.

The air was cool and damp, swaddling the day's first sounds against the outside world.

His arms pulled against the leather tack, and Thunderbolt leapt a chasm.

They raced the final fifty meters to the mesa's flat crest, where Casmir brought the animal to a halt.

Man and beast stood still, the gray morning mist forming twisted clouds that hung in the stagnant air, the thunderhoof's exhalations coming as blowing cones of gauzy vapor.

The animal was more horse than buffalo, muscular, with a coat as gray as slate. The party that had originally encountered them had branded them with the name *thunderhoof* for the way the herd's retreat had sounded as it reverberated through the valley. It was an apt name. The animals populated the wide green plains on this planet, and there were some among the U3 community who thought the thunderhoofs had some limited form of intelligence—or at least a keener consciousness than the animals on Earth had expressed. Casmir didn't really agree with this—though he was happy to have his people study these creatures, as well as others on the planet, more closely.

The thunderhoofs seemed to communicate their basic desires through a series of movements and sounds made through their mouths and through a blow hole at the back of their skulls. After realizing this, Universe Three's citizens had come to an oddly capitalistic relationship with the beasts in which the human population provided the animals with food and grooming in return for services that included towing, simple transportation, and in Casmir's case, recreation.

Thunderbolt rolled its muscles over one shoulder and vocalized a sputtering sound.

Casmir looked in the direction the beast suggested, and saw a pair of birds of a species he had never seen before. The colony had been on the planet for nine local years, which translated to more than seven Earth standards, but they still had a lot to learn.

"Beautiful," he said out loud as he rubbed the thunderhoof's shoulder to thank him for bringing the birds to his attention.

The land spread out below them in greens and browns. Only a few of the buildings of what his people now called Atropos City were lighted at this hour, and of those only a few trailed smoke or heated water vapor from their ceiling ducts and electric generators. Universe Three had considered several names for their capitol, but once it was public knowledge that the earliest UG raiders had used Atropos City as an ironic name for their little dirt bowl of a settlement, the board unanimously agreed to adopt the name.

Atropos City.

Casmir liked it for its aspiration.

The name gave him and his people a target. A goal.

From its rudimentary beginnings, the people of Universe Three would create a city and then a population and then an entire set of civilizations that the United Government could never understand.

He smiled at that, then looked to the east where Lake Miyear reflected the first rays of Eta Cass as an orange bolt that creased the water's surface.

Casmir drew a breath and looked at the industrial complex that was beginning to sprawl across the northern landscape. Technical people went to work in those buildings—designers, engineers, controllers, assembly techs, and welders. And even better, physicists—including the brilliant Jorge Catazara—the best and brightest mind that money, personal bravery, and the ideals of true personal freedom could acquire.

A skimmer raced across the land below.

Rail lines ran into the complex from the south and the west now, connecting up the foundry to the early mines that Kazima Yamada had been building. A half-filled trolley was still being unloaded after its evening delivery of metal-laced ore that would be smelted and used in the manufacture of machines they needed to build even more impressive machines.

Star Drive spaceships.

They had been able to build standard space-faring craft for the past two years, but it had taken them longer to get to this point where they could piece together the sophisticated manufacturing tools it took to make a Star Drive engine. They were close—so very close. Maybe even next fall they would be able to build their own fleet modeled after the hand-built prototypes they had already managed.

The complex was a beautiful sight.

Casmir was one of the few people of Universe Three who still kept the Solar System standard calendar in his memory, and in a few days he would cross his sixtieth standard birthday. That meant he had been working with the group who had become U3 for just over forty years.

It was a hard number to swallow.

Ah, Perigee, he thought. *How I wish you could see this.*

The communications pad on his belt rumbled.

He gritted his teeth at the interruption.

"Yes," he said.

"Sorry to disturb you, sir, but Deidra said we should contact you immediately." It was Martin Scalese, the man who operated the communications center.

"Perhaps she was wrong," he snapped.

"I apologize again, sir."

Casmir scoffed at himself then.

"It's all right, Martin. It is not your fault that my daughter is so fervent in her views."

"No, sir. I guess not."

Of his children, Casmir wasn't surprised Deidra had been the one to take to the organization. She believed in it fully, but at almost twenty-one years old she was going through the early stage of radical exuberance that was always marked by high verbal temperatures and knee-jerk reactions.

"So, what is it?"

"We've received a communication."

"Yes?"

"From the United Government."

He paused. Even though it had been several weeks since *Everguard* had been destroyed, the UG had not yet directly responded. He had begun to worry, but he hadn't considered the idea that they might attempt to contact them directly.

"How did it come in?"

"Standard radio, sir. We assume they jumped *Orion* into our system, sent the message, and then jumped back out."

"What does it say?"

"Are you sitting down, sir?"

Casmir glanced at the thunderhoof's gray back, then out over the distance.

"You could say that," he said.

CHAPTER 3

Aldrin Station
Local Date: January 19, 2215
Local Time: 1940

Lieutenant Commander Torrance Black walked into the admiral's office.

It was mid second shift. His brain was mushy from seven hours lost in deep thought, but the mere act of doing that work had brought a new sense of purpose to his step. He would crash later, but for the moment he felt oddly energized.

The admiral's desk was a translucent block of smoky black glass inlaid with an ornate design of cherry wood. The wall behind her was a display panel in dark blue marked with the flags of Interstellar Command and the United Government. Soft ceiling lighting reflected off a floor of white tiles. Two men, visitors, sat on hard chairs beside the desk, one in admiral's whites, the other in a green jumper with mission patches stitched along his arm. Flair at his collar marked him as a captain.

The admiral came from behind the desk to greet Torrance.

Naomi Umaro's frame was tall and trim—a form accentuated by her crisp white uniform. Her heritage was hard to pick out, part Mediterranean, part Scandinavian, maybe some Malay. She wore her black hair pulled back from her face. It was going gray along one temple. Her skin was smooth over her cheekbones, but a slight crinkle of crow's feet gathered at the corners of her eyes to suggest that she was maybe ten standards older than Torrance.

The decoration swath set at her collarbone was meshed with the shimmering icons that marked her service history, a history built of short stints in multiple spaceports—a trajectory that said Umaro was an officer with both a plan and enough backing within the command to make that plan happen.

She had been groomed for this role, and seemed more than comfortable in her own skin. Rumors said she had larger political roles in her future, and Torrance saw nothing in this first impression to argue otherwise.

"Thank you for coming," she said as they shook hands. "How's the wrist?"

"You're welcome," he replied, holding up the soft wrap. He had broken it during the *Everguard* sabotage. "Doctor says I'll be out of this in a day or two, so I guess I'm doing fine."

"Can I get you anything? Coffee? Sandwich?"

"No thank you. I grabbed a sandwich on the way over."

"Then please have a seat." The admiral motioned him to a soft-backed chair, then sat on the edge of her desk as he settled in.

"Let me introduce Rear Admiral Ihiri Montague and Captain Wallace Douglas."

"Good afternoon," Torrance said.

"It is an honor to meet you," the rear admiral replied.

Douglas gave a toothless smile and nodded politely.

Rear Admiral Montague was short in his chair, and a little too rounded in the middle, probably from a few too many state dinners. But he was crisply dressed, and carried his power in the casual way of an elder statesman.

Douglas was altogether different.

His eyes were brown lasers. The curve of his nose lent him an aura of hawkishness, and his jawline was square and chiseled enough to cut glass. His light brown skin was scarred to nearly nonexistent pebble along his right cheek. Torrance wondered if he had been burned.

"Do you have any idea why I asked you here, Commander?" Umaro asked.

"I couldn't say."

Her grin was warm but did nothing to make him feel better. Then he realized what she had just said.

"Commander?"

"I signed your orders this morning. That is, if you want them. I understand you were planning to decommission."

Torrance glanced at the men, then back to Umaro.

"I'm not sure what to say."

She crossed her arms and leaned back with an expression that was a mixture of smugness and charm. "We pulled four hundred and fifty-three people off *Everguard* because of you, Commander."

"I had help from my team."

"You were the leader."

Torrance nodded. That was the gig. If the team did well, the leader was brilliant, if not, the leader was crap.

"Your record is otherwise solid, but not particularly noteworthy. A single reprimand, never repeated, and an ill-fated attempt to save an indeterminate life-form."

Since Captain Romanov suggested he was keeping that detail off Torrance's record, he was surprised Umaro knew of this. But rather than fear repercussions, Torrance was now torn between being gutted by Umaro's matter-of-fact tone as she said the words *not particularly noteworthy* and feeling something that approached giddiness when he imagined how Government Security Officer Casey would be gagging if he were here to see Torrance offered a promotion.

Umaro continued. "But the fact is that you were the Officer of Record who solved a critical technical problem and launched the wormhole pods that changed the world. That makes you important. And what you did on *Everguard* makes you a hero. Every kid in the Solar System knows the name Torrance Black now."

"For better or for worse?" Torrance asked.

Umaro ignored the comment.

"You deserve the promotion for that alone."

Torrance moved his fingers to feel the residual pain in his hand.

Umaro continued.

"But the fact you're a hero is not what made your papers easy to sign, Torrance. To be totally honest, every person in the service is a potential hero if the situation lines up just so. And, while the media is focusing on your efforts to take down Lieutenant Malloy, we both know that bravery in the line of fire doesn't have a lot to say about whether a person makes a great leader or not." She paused. "I've processed paperwork for a lot of heroes whose promotions I didn't think were particularly wise. But what made your orders easy to sign is that every crew member in System Command that day said that your leadership under pressure is what saved lives aboard that ship."

An image of Karl Malloy flashed across his mind.

Malloy, his compatriot who had been a U3 mole. Malloy, the man who set the explosive charges that resulted in *Everguard*'s destruction and some two thousand deaths.

"We didn't save everyone."

Admiral Montague cleared his throat. "You saved everyone who could be saved, Commander," he said.

Torrance's agreement was only a faint nod.

Commander, he thought.

He hadn't expected that. The rank sounded odd on his tongue as he pretended to say it. Three syllables instead of six. Strange. He sat back in his chair, still on alert but taking in the three of them.

Umaro's gaze was firm.

The other two men sat in their chairs, waiting like gamblers at a horse race.

"There's more to this, isn't there?" he asked.

"I need you to do something for me," Umaro replied.

The temperature of the room dropped.

"I want you to accept an assignment to the Eta Cass system."

"Eta Cass?" he said.

"That's where Universe Three has set up shop," Umaro replied.

Understanding dawned.

Universe Three had been jumping *Icarus* and *Einstein* into the Solar System to pick people up—or kidnap people, if you believed certain news outlets—and transport them to whatever base of operations they had set up. Torrance had also heard gossip about an operation the United Government had run against the terrorists after Starburst, but he had never seen anything official about it.

"You've just given me classified information."

"As of this morning, you're cleared."

"Wasn't that presumptuous?"

"Was it?"

Her gaze cut into him. The world around him began moving a little too fast.

"We're going to retaliate?"

Umaro shook her head.

She slid from the corner of her desk and moved to stand behind her chair, her long fingers curled over its edge as she leaned against its back.

"That's what everyone expects us to do, isn't it? The press is reporting the loss of *Everguard* put the war is back into 'hot' mode, so I'm sure everyone expects us to go in guns blazing."

Torrance felt the intensity of the captain and the rear admiral as she spoke.

"But the supreme president has decided to go a different way. We're going to attempt to bring this violence to an end by sending a negotiating team to Eta Cass."

"We're giving up?"

"Is that frustration in your voice?"

"I'm sorry if that was inappropriate."

"I understand frustration, Torrance."

"We all do," Captain Douglas added from the side.

A flicker of annoyance came across Umaro's gaze as she stepped around the chair and took her seat again. She was clearly upset by the Douglas's ad lib, but by the time she spoke, her expression was back under control.

"We want to discuss our common goals."

"Do we have common goals?"

"Universe Three is small enough that they can't afford to lose people, and with our full manufacturing capability still a standard year away, we can't afford to lose equipment."

Torrance gripped the arm of his seat with his good hand.

He didn't like discussing loss of life as if it was nothing but a bargaining chip. It was that kind of truth telling that made him uncomfortable with the service.

"You've been at flight on *Everguard* for the past fifteen standards, Commander," Umaro said. "Which means you have no way to fully understand what it's like to fight this kind of interstellar war. They jump in, pound our forces while they kidnap our people, and then get out before we can jump *Orion* in to defend them. U3 understands these missions—they know precisely how long it takes a warning call to travel from their target to Kensington, which is where we station *Orion* because that's the optimally shortest distance from what our intel officers consider to be U3's primary targets. That means they have a window for every op. They've been precise about it—just under an hour on-station around Jupiter, less than twenty minutes at Mars, jumps to Ceres are timed to last under ten minutes."

"Impressive," Torrance said.

"It is, isn't it?" Montague replied.

Umaro continued. "The only advantage we have is that we can guess the mission window of every op they are likely to run."

Douglas leaned into the conversation. "Which is like telling a kid that a holiday lasts twenty-four hours, but not letting him know what day it falls on."

Umaro didn't hide her glare this time.

"In the meantime," Montague added, attempting to steer the conversation back onto track, "we can't jump *Orion* out to attack them in their own home system because our bean counters are frozen with worry that we might lose her."

"Which we might," Umaro snapped.

"There appears to be discord in the chicken coop," Torrance more mumbled than said.

"What's that?"

"Nothing," he replied. "Just something my dad used to say back when I was a kid."

His dad had always tried too hard to be an earthy kind of a guy when in reality he was just an ordinary day worker, watching over robots, checking their programming, and doing quality control on their work. In some ways not much different from Torrance, really.

Umaro looked Torrance in the eye.

"If you get the idea that opening a negotiation with Universe Three isn't setting well with everyone, you're on point. Some think we should throw everything we've got into obliterating Atropos—which is where Universe Three has their home base. But most of our strategists say that even if we had the firepower to destroy U3—which we don't, not yet anyway—well, they say the galaxy is too damned big."

"Too many places to hide," Torrance said.

"Right. We think Universe Three's leadership has already put people in several other locations around the Eta Cass system."

"That would make sense," Torrance said. "Spreading their people would keep us from being able to destroy them in one blast."

"Exactly."

She glanced at Rear Admiral Montague, hesitating long enough for him to give a gesture that was half a shrug and half an expression of You're On Your Own.

"Those same analysts say Francis is probably building his own Star Drive engines, too."

The idea took Torrance back. "They're copying us," he said.

"Of course."

"They're stealing our scientists, too," Douglas burst in.

"Bottom line," Umaro said, "our analysts think that any attempt to crush them will result in Universe Three shuffling off to another planet and growing more resistant. They think a display of force would essentially strengthen U3's will to dig in. Given the cost of war on a galactic scale, the supreme president has decided we can't afford to keep throwing money into this situation. This is our chance to bring a peaceful resolution to this whole thing."

The muscles along Douglas's jaw rippled. He shifted in his seat but didn't say anything.

"We are military," Umaro said in response to the captain's body language. "We don't make policy, we enact it. So our intention is to jump *Orion* into U3's system and ask Casmir Francis to board us for negotiations."

"With all due respect, Admiral," Torrance said. "I can't imagine anyone from U3 would step aboard a United Government Star Drive cruiser right now."

"That's among the reasons we intend to meet on their turf."

Her expression indicated she thought she had answered his question.

"We've already broadcast the request," she continued. "Ambassador Reyes will arrive on station within a standard week. Assuming Francis agrees to our offer, the mission will launch shortly thereafter."

"And if he doesn't agree?"

Umaro shrugged. "Then that's someone else's problem."

Torrance pursed his lips. "I see."

And he did. No one in this room had any idea of what was really going to happen. He rubbed his sore hand absently.

Umaro seemed to be spent, Montague perplexed, and Douglas was just sitting there grinding his teeth to nubs.

"So," Torrance said. "What do I have to do with this?"

Umaro gave a churlish grin.

"We're struggling with a technical problem—integrating our newest weapon systems with *Orion*'s shipboard controllers. It needs to be working now if we're going to protect our crew. You're the highest-profile systems leader we've got. I want you to lead a technical team under Captain Douglas here. I intend to put you in charge of both Weapons and Systems. Make this happen, and I doubt commander will be your last stop."

You're the highest-profile systems leader we've got? What did that mean?

"H-MADS?" Torrance said.

It stood for Hallway Multithreat Analysis and Defense System. If the tech notes were accurate, H-MADS was a remotely monitored security system designed to use sensor feeds from hallways and chambers inside the ship to trigger defensive action.

Torrance's skin grew cold.

"You're prepared to gun people down on the ship?"

"I see you've been reading your technical notes."

Montague leaned forward in his perch.

"Inviting U3 delegates aboard one of our spacecraft leaves us open to attack, Commander Black," he said. "You see that, right? Especially if we open our doors to U3's security personnel—which we assume will be necessary in order to ensure their leadership is comfortable. If you recall, the U3 security group knows everything about our Excelsior ship's basic systems. We've upgraded several elements of it, but it's safest to assume they've kept up with us."

"You assume U3 has people in our ranks?"

"Of course we do," Douglas said, the muscles of his jaw flexing. The captain clearly did not want Torrance on his team.

"*Everguard* alone proves that's the best assumption," Umaro added.

"That still doesn't answer 'why me?' I mean, I'm out of date. I don't know anything about modern systems."

The admiral swiveled back in her chair. Her white jacket was stark against the soft leather of the seat. Montague sat straight and stiff. Douglas shifted with a satisfied grin that let Torrance know the captain had made this exact same argument earlier.

"Having you there closes the loop."

Torrance swallowed hard, thinking about what that answer meant. "You want me because it makes a great story."

Umaro raised one long finger. "You're getting this opportunity because your background puts you in a position to command respect, and," she extended a second finger, "you have proven you can keep your cool in tense situations." She put her hand down. "But like it or not, you stand for something now. When you walk into a room your crewmates see a man who managed a tense situation, a man who understood his spacecraft, and a man who became responsible for saving hundreds of lives."

He pursed his lips.

"That's how it works, Torrance. Your skills are your ticket into the game, but a lot of people can acquire technical skills whereas not many can really lead. There are people in this command who would literally kill to have been in the position you found yourself in. You rose to a challenge. Entire careers are made of the kind of thing you just did."

He hadn't thought of it that way.

"So, while all three of us fully acknowledge that the PR you can bring to a *successful* mission has value beyond my ability to measure, I want you to understand that I'm not promoting you because you bring a crowd. I'm promoting you because I see your ability to get things done, and because I need your leadership on that ship."

"I see."

"This is your chance, Torrance." Umaro intertwined her fingers and put her hands flat on the table before her as she leaned forward to stare directly at him. "This is your chance to be that one person who changes everything."

Torrance frowned at Umaro's quoting the chaplain. He flexed his mending hand and felt stiffness breaking away. The dull pain felt good. It felt right. The sleeve of his uniform carried the now-obsolete insignia of lieutenant commander. He thought about Marisa Harthing, lying in her hospital room, and about Thomas Kitchell, who would be released soon. He thought about friends who had died on *Everguard*, his teammates who had been hurt.

The impression of the data crystal in his pocket was a bump against his hip.

The military had been his life for a long time now. He had been purposefully ignoring the anxiety that came with the idea of decommissioning because he didn't really know what he was going to do next. The idea of finding a peaceful solution to this whole mess was tantalizing.

And, quite honestly, it felt very good to be wanted.

"Will I still be able to study Alpha Centauri A's signals?" he said.

"When you return?" the admiral asked.

"Of course." He had waited years, what was a little longer?

"I don't see any reason you shouldn't. In fact, I would expect your role might give you access to expertise that might help you." Her smile showed only a touch of condescension. "I would ask that you go through a standard peer-review process before making any statements, though."

He gave a close-lipped nod of his head, considering.

She held her hand out over the desk, palm open. "Do we have a deal?"

He paused, then shook it.

"All I've ever wanted to do was to serve," he said.

But that was wrong. He knew it the moment he said it. Marisa had been right all those years ago. Military service fit his personality, but Torrance Black had not wanted to *serve*. He had *wanted* to be exceptional. All his life he had wanted to be able to tell himself he made a difference. He wanted to be something more than a cog in the machine.

Until now, he had never really understood that.

CHAPTER 4

Atropos, Eta Cassiopeia System
Local Date: Studna 23, 9
Local Time: 0535

Giving Thunderbolt a final pat of appreciation, Casmir rode across the plot of land the people of Atropos City called the corral. It was a field where thunderhoofs and humans interacted, a few hundred meters per side and bordered by a pair of fences that had been built to mark boundaries rather than restrain movement. The ground here was more hard dirt than grass.

"Treat him well," he said to the stable hand as he came to a halt and slipped out of the saddle.

The girl was maybe ten years old.

"I will, Director," she said.

"I know you will," he replied.

She gave him a confused look. "Are you all right?"

"I'm fine," he replied. "Why do you ask?"

"You left the bit in."

He blushed, and went back to the animal. The stable hand would have handled it for anyone else, but Casmir had made a point of doing it himself and he was a stickler for this kind of detail.

"I'm sorry, old friend," he said as he removed the harness. "I find myself suddenly distracted this morning."

Thunderbolt didn't react to the words, but the animal pulled back when Casmir ran his hand over his forehead.

The animal, it seemed, was also a creature of habit.

Casmir made a clicking sound from the back of his throat.

It was a tone of frustration more than anything else, because there was no way to explain to the animal what the mere idea of the United Government's willingness to discuss independence meant to him. Not that the animal would have understood.

After removing the harness, Casmir left Thunderbolt to the girl. She would see he was groomed and had a proper feeding if he wanted it, then she would leave the animal free to rejoin the herd and spend the rest of the morning doing whatever it was that these creatures did.

He stomped toward the Castle. Eta Cass had fully risen now and cast sharp-edged shadows across the ground. The smell of the land and the sight of the open sky reminded him of a time when he and Yvonne had traveled to Earth's Australia, but the big-fronded trees and the unique smell of the nearby river brought him firmly back to this place and this time.

Universe Three had been here long enough that this was now home.

The comparison made him smile, though.

Atropos City and the Australian outback.

An interesting pairing.

Casmir walked on.

His home was a building the people of Universe Three had built for him in the first months of their colony's existence. They took to calling it the Castle almost immediately, which made him uncomfortable at the time, but which had grown on him to the point where he found he liked the name as long as it was said with just the right amount of sarcasm. Universe Three had built onto it since those early days, though, and in some ways it now seemed like much more of its name-sake than he was really happy with.

He pulled a leather glove off one hand as he strode past the security gate, and was working on the other when the door to the main building opened.

"It's a trick," Deidra said, stepping out with an entourage of security personnel right behind.

She was shorter than Casmir, and slighter, looking a great deal like Yvonne had in her younger days but with blond hair. She strutted boldly out to meet him, that long hair gleaming almost white in the early light.

"Good morning, my wonderful daughter," he replied.

"I'm telling you, it's a trick."

He strode with her through the foyer and into the central corridor, where Martin Scalese and a collection of guards had gathered to escort them. The governing board would already have been assembled in what the group had taken to calling the Exchange Room, the large assembly area that spanned almost all of the building's upper floor.

"Perhaps it *is* a trick," Casmir replied, "but what is it that makes you think so?"

"Isn't it obvious?"

Casmir glared at her as they walked. "I want you to tell me what you're thinking."

Her words came in bunches as she kept up with his strides.

"The UG doesn't roll over and play dead, Papa. You know that better than anyone. They never have and they never will. We've developed and reviewed so many strategies regarding their tactics that there's nothing left to review, right? In all that time, we've never—never—spent even a minute discussing the idea of a UG surrender."

They made their way up a wide stairway.

"And that's because?"

"We all know it just plain won't happen."

"Perhaps we were wrong."

"No, Papa. The UG cannot be trusted. We can't meet them like this."

"If what you say is true, there will *never* be a way to bring this to a close."

"Maybe there isn't."

"That would be very sad."

"We should be strong, Papa. We should take their offer and tell them to shove it right up—"

Casmir raised his hand to cut her off as they came to the top of the stairway. A pair of double doors made of dark wood led to the Exchange Room.

In the dim light of the hallway, Casmir took in his daughter's expression. Her lips were drawn tight. Her jaw set. Fire burned in her watery blue eyes that were so much like her mother's.

"You are young, Deidra. Aggressive and bold. I like that in a person who I know will one day be leading our people. But you know exactly how serious I am about how we make decisions. You also know I've learned many lessons in my time—and among the main lessons I've learned is that Ellyn was right when she taught us that we have to be able to engage the system to defeat it. Engage it on the fringes, yes, but still engage it. I didn't listen to that part of her message before. I tried to force things from completely outside the United Government's control. All that got us is an adversary who has not yet destroyed us, but only because we managed to strike first and because we are lucky enough to be farther away than its arms can comfortably reach."

"It got us all this," she said.

Casmir stopped. He used his gaze to halt his daughter.

"We were very lucky," he said. "You need to always keep in mind that one misstep along the way would have meant our entire way of life could have been destroyed."

Her eyes narrowed. "That's why we need to attack now, Papa. Take it to them while they are weak."

Casmir shook his head.

"Perhaps you are right," he said, putting his hand on the door handle. "But there are other options to discuss, first."

Then Casmir pushed open the door and stepped into a large room.

———

To his left, the Exchange Room's wall was solid and expansive, but the other three were mostly open windows, a fact that gave the area a greater sense of spaciousness than it might have deserved. The frames around those windows were load-bearing columns of rough mudbrick painted a brownish-yellow shade that reminded Casmir of the mustard his agricultural people once made from mold back when they lived on Mars. The day outside was pleasant, so the storm shades were pulled. Natural light flooded the room, and a gentle breeze kept things cool.

The staff was all here, all seated around a central table which was long, curved, and bent into a hemisphere focused on the center of the wall to Casmir's left. They were all engaged in a collection of scattered conversations.

Casmir strode to the front and center of the room and put his fingertips on the tabletop. Deidra followed behind him at first, but peeled off to fill the lone empty seat around the table.

Gregor Anderson, Casmir's oldest and most trusted confidante, was the first to notice his presence. Seated at the center of the table, he squared his chair and turned a comfortable gaze in Casmir's direction. He had been speaking with Professor Catazara, who also grew quiet, though didn't react with any particular sense of purpose. For the first time in a while, Casmir noticed how the years had changed his friend —took in the lines that ran over Gregor's forehead, and the fact that his beard had gone from dusty gray to nearly pure white a few locals ago.

The conversations dwindled until only a single animated conversation filled the room. This, too, came to an end when Gregor made an obvious motion with his hand.

"Sorry about that," the man said to everyone.

Timmon Keyes, the U3 captain of *Icarus*, sat next to Brooke Nassir, a weapons expert who had recently taken command of *Einstein*. They both gave bemused gazes.

"I assume you've all heard the news," Casmir said.

Gregor replied for the group with his gravelly voice.

"We know the United Government has requested a parlay to discuss our future."

"It's a trick," Deidra said.

Casmir gave her an exasperated glare.

"Does anyone need a grown daughter?" he quipped. There was light laughter. "She comes partially trained, but with a full set of opinions." The laughter this time was more pronounced and took a moment to quiet down.

Deidra's expression said she was not amused.

Casmir shrugged and raised his palms with a *what are you going to do* expression. Then he stood taller and paced to the far side of the room.

"We need options," he said. "We need to discuss all ideas, and we need to discuss them now."

Kazima Yamada sat forward in her seat, folded her fingers together, then rested her chin on the points of her extended index fingers. "I don't think we should do anything," she said.

Yamada had always been Casmir's most favored adviser on various engineering systems, and she had been instrumental in devising the escape plan that the colony had used to shuttle off of Mars. Now she was leading the build-out of Atropos City's manufacturing plants. She was also, however, a woman with a high degree of interest in and knowledge about political maneuvering. Casmir had often bounced ideas off her.

"Why do you say that?" he replied.

"Because if it isn't broken, you don't fix it. We've got a two-ship-to-one advantage. I don't see any reason to risk that now."

"The UG isn't just playing humble dog," Deidra said. "If what Intel is reporting is true, they'll be able to build more Star Drives within a year, anyway."

"As will we," Yamada replied.

"Gregor?" Casmir said.

Gregor rubbed his finger and thumb through his beard. "You've seen the reports on their manufacturing capability," he said. "I can't imagine it will be more than a year."

"And our own ships will be coming off the production line in less than two months," Yamada replied.

"You know I'm on your side, Kazima," Gregor replied. "But that's an aggressive estimate, and even if it's right, the UG has the people and resources of the entire Solar System at its disposal. We've got one planet and several thousand citizens."

Yamada grimaced, but it was clear she understood and even agreed with Gregor's assessment of the situation. Universe Three could never keep pace with the Uglies' ability to produce.

"To do nothing would eventually put us into a position of weakness," Deidra said. She seemed ready to come out of her seat, but somehow managed to keep her conversation to a degree of calmness that surprised Casmir.

Yamada nodded sagely. "Then our only real option is to accept their offer—"

"There are other options," Deidra replied.

"Ms. Yamada has the floor," Casmir said.

The room froze. The clackety sound of the city below filtered in through the windows.

"Go ahead, Kazima," Casmir said. "How would we proceed if we meet with them."

"I don't know," she said, sheepishly. "We have to think about it. But my first thought is that we would send both *Icarus* and *Einstein* to the session."

"Both with weapons trained on *Orion* in case something unexpected happens," Keyes added. He glanced at Nassir, who nodded back.

"Right," Yamada said. "We have a numerical advantage. We should use it."

"If we do that, I suggest not telling the UG team which ship our negotiating party would be on," Gregor said.

"I would be on that team," Casmir said.

"That's a bad idea," Gregor shot back.

"I'm not letting someone else take a risk I'm not willing to take myself."

"No one would think anything about that."

"Yes, they would," Casmir said.

"It's not wise," Gregor replied.

"I'll be all right," Casmir said. He turned to his daughter. "What do you think of that idea?"

"I think they'll kill you," she said.

"But if they do not," he replied, "it could mean the beginning of a truly free system for us."

Deidra crossed her arms.

Petulant, Casmir thought. That word was designed for Deidra.

"We could add some insurance," Yamada said.

"What do you mean?"

"I like having both ships scrambled. But I think we should also make it known that we have something on each of the ships that's important to them."

"What are you suggesting?" Gregor said.

"Captives," Casmir said as a full understanding of what Yamada was proposing came over him. "You're suggesting we put captives on each ship."

"Human shields?" Deidra said.

"Not human shields," Yamada said. "Rewards."

Casmir strolled to the far side of the room and stared out the window. The streets below him pulsed with movement. Yamada's idea gave him a nervous chill, but it made sense.

"Yes," he said. "We can communicate it as a gift, a civilized present for agreeing to speak with us. Suggest to the UG that we appreciate the opportunity to work as equals, and as such offer to transport some of their people to *Orion* as soon as our discussions are completed."

"That would be brilliant," Yamada said.

Casmir turned to his friend. "Gregor?"

The elder Anderson sat back and took in a contemplative breath. "I think it could work."

"But you're not certain?"

"It's the United Government we're talking about—they have a citizenship to govern, and they haven't been winning. We shouldn't assume anything for certain."

Heads around the table nodded.

"On the other hand," Gregor said, "retrieving their captives gives them something to spin to their advantage. If they get another concession or two, they could make it look good for themselves."

"I can't believe we're talking about this," Deidra said.

"You would have us destroy *Orion* on sight?" Casmir said.

"It's the safest play."

He scanned the room. Deidra's view had its supporters. Kyleen Lian, the group's agricultural director, seemed particularly inclined to support the idea, but then, Kyleen had always taken interest in Deidra's progress, and Casmir was not certain that interest was completely professional.

"If we destroy *Orion*, it gives us a span of ultimate control," Deidra said. "I know how cold that sounds, but it's a circumstance that may never happen again. A chance to be the only force in the universe with faster-than-light capability. We could use that window to shut down their entire program. I understand that sounds harsh, but the United Government has done far worse things under the guise of *societal progress*."

Casmir hid a grimace at Deidra's twisting of the "the other side is far worse" argument that Ellyn Parker had once used in her recruiting campaigns back in the days when Universe Three was just a college activist's dream.

He scanned his leadership team. "Are there any other options?"

No one responded.

"All right, then," he said.

He went to a pressure board and used the tip of his finger to physically write as he talked.

"We seem to have three choices. One: Ignore the request and go on. The obvious downside to this is that eventually the UG will achieve the ability to build more Star Drives. When that happens their production capability will dwarf ours. Then we could be in a position of weakness."

He finished writing, and then scanned the room.

When there were no questions, he turned back to the board.

"Two: We meet them and try to become equals. If the offer is a ruse, the UG could use the situation to ambush our ships and disable our leadership—but we can mitigate that with the idea of offering them their captives back."

He checked back with the team.

"And, three: Attack their ship immediately. The downside here is that overt aggression for the sake of aggression will almost certainly lead to a more intense war sometime in the future…unless victory is complete. In which case, we can make immense short-term headway."

He turned back one last time.

"Does that capture it all?"

"It does," Gregor said.

"All right then," Casmir said, stretching his neck to the left and the right. "I would say it's time to vote."

CHAPTER 5

UGIS *Orion*
Local Date: January 24, 2215
Local Time: 0600

Word came through an ultrasecure channel the next morning.

Universe Three had accepted.

Between taking care of a few personal details, Torrance crammed information about this new spacecraft into his mind for two days before arriving at his post. He committed as much of each system interface into his memory as he could manage, absorbed every important element of every spec he could find. But in the end, it was all too much too fast.

As he stepped onto *Orion*'s mission deck and into his first technical problem, he felt completely overwhelmed.

The ship's H-MADS—Hallway Multithreat Analysis and Defense System—was fouled up.

H-MADS was conceived after the Starburst fiasco, which had been predicated on Universe Three using moles to capture *Einstein* and *Icarus*. The system's operational profile—the algorithms it used to monitor activity and take action to shut down insurgency at a moment's notice—were devised by a well-paid UG think tank.

Orion had been outfitted with the H-MADS as soon as it had been developed, but the system had never really worked right and her commanding officers had ordered it turned off years ago for fear it would do more harm than good. Now it had been brought back, reconfigured and reinstalled in the past two weeks under the cloak of a simple operations refit.

Given the time, *Orion*'s corridors were nearly empty.

Which was good. Torrance was still feeling overwhelmed, and it was nice to have a few minutes to reacquaint himself to the ship.

Which, of course, he used up in thinking about the H-MADS problem. In the end, he was pleased to have something like this to focus on. At least with shipboard systems there was always an answer: Things either worked or they didn't. Unlike wars, politics, or business, which got more convoluted the more you knew, shipboard systems were always clean and simple at their heart. Eventually, anyway.

As he thought, he kept in mind the old idea that a good system commander walks through a ship as if he owns it.

His gait was steady.

Crisp steps of an easy rhythm.

Where his old ship was built on a circular pattern and felt rounded everywhere, *Orion* was full of corners. Gravity System Command was further down the hallway, and P2—the secondary propulsion system monitoring station—was back the other way. Torrance glanced at the doorways as he passed, trying to find familiar landmarks and commit images to memory.

As Torrance passed the propulsion center he strained to see past the front offices, hoping to glimpse the cylindrical wormhole drives he had heard so much about. He wanted to see the Star Drive system with his own eyes. He wanted to watch the exotic matter generators spin at near superluminal while they pushed energy into microquantum tunnels that existed for only the barest of moments in time—or, perhaps didn't exist at all, if you believed one of the more eccentric theories about what was actually happening.

The exotic matter generators were the secret to it all.

Mathematical beauty, quantum style.

But Torrance wasn't here to manage propulsion systems.

He was here to deal with the integration of shipboard and weapon systems, which, until he had spent the time digging deeper into H-MADS, even he had admitted was an interesting pairing.

When he turned a corner and arrived at the H-MADS post, three of his team were gathered in the hallway just under the place where a smooth sensor bulge grew from the ceiling. Each wore *Orion*'s green jumpers and system test belts. They had pulled a panel from the inner wall and were pointing into the open hole and arguing at enough volume that their voices were carrying. The processing unit inside lay exposed with bare wire, optical fiber, and RF sensors hanging from the equipment like snakes in a mechanical Medusa's hair. Torrance recognized the optical processing chipset from his morning's reading.

"So this is H-MADS, eh?" he said.

Their argument came to an abrupt halt.

"Sir!" A young man straightened to informal attention. It was Lieutenant Arthur Skiles.

Torrance took in the team.

Skiles was the systems interface leader. Lieutenant Junior Grade Angela Ramista was a shared software developer, and Lieutenant Mia Kluvac, the optical systems coordinator.

"Where's Yuan?" he said.

Skiles hesitated for an awkward moment, still at attention.

"At ease, please," Torrance said.

All three came down from attention, but none of them were truly at ease.

Torrance wasn't blind to the idea that his reputation would precede him, but the effect would be even stronger with crewmates under his command—they would be dealing with a double dose of uncertainty: a new commander, and a new commander who was a media hero. He wanted to get off on the right foot.

"This might be a tough way to get introduced, but it kind of works for me, all right?" Torrance said. "At the core, I'm just an engineer, exactly like you guys."

"Yes, sir," Skiles said.

"So you can help me get started by calling me Commander, or in our most informal moments you can probably get away with a simple Torrance. I'm not going to bite anyone who's working hard."

"Thank you, Commander."

Skiles relaxed.

"So, where's Yuan?"

"I don't know, sir."

"I would think she would be here."

LiJuan Yuan had been the chief weapon systems officer. As a result of Admiral Umaro's assignment, however, she now reported directly through Torrance, a fact that she had clearly taken as a demotion, a reaction that was as predictable as it was appropriate. No officer wants to move backward on the scorecard. The fact that he understood why she would be upset did not, however, mean he had to be any happier to deal with the fallout, and the reputation that preceded her didn't help any. Every performance report he read about Yuan said she was brilliant and infinitely capable, but was also a person with fixed opinions who could be hard to deal with if you didn't see things her way. He could already hear her excuses. *"It is a systems issue, not a problem with my weapons,"* she would explain in a tone that would hold a clear undercurrent of her contempt for the situation.

Skiles ran a nervous palm down the side of his jumper. He was a kid, really—twenty-four years old with an unlined face and a shock of hair as dark as a black hole. His age made Torrance think of Thomas Kitchell, but Skiles's pedigree was as different from Kitchell's as a diamond's was from coal. Arthur Skiles made his mark early by graduating from the academy in only three years. His focus was in control systems and automation. Where Kitchell had been a bit of a snot-nosed idiot until he grew comfortable in the team, Skiles had a quick smile and a natural tendency to draw people to him. He had lettered on the track team.

He was supposed to be good at what he did.

"I don't know where she is," Skiles said. "We don't seem to hook up very well sometimes."

Ramista and Kluvac shuffled their feet and did their best *I'm not really here* imitations, so he didn't press the point.

"Show me the problem, Lieutenant," Torrance said.

Skiles pointed to a display tacked to the wall.

"We've followed the test procedure exactly. The sequence is on cube —meaning we're feeding false video to the sensor algorithm to test it."

He toggled the test sequence.

The system was supposed to gather video from the hallway sensor, then pass it to a distributed computer which would compare the data stream to items in a threat library. The system analyzed language, movement, and objects to categorize the moment. If H-MADS saw the situation as dangerous, H-MADS was supposed to engage whatever weapon systems were nearby, and deliver alerts in whatever manner was appropriate.

Torrance watched the video monitor as it pumped the false image of a drone robot wearing a service jumper and deck boots entering the hallway. H-MADS registered its presence. Everything seemed to be fine.

"Now watch," Skiles said.

The robot's arm swung upward as if to scratch its head. The H-MADS threat analysis program recorded the movement and incorrectly assessed it as aggressive, then engaged the local energy beam. Laser weapons clicked on a moment later. If Skiles hadn't followed proper safety protocol and deactivated the weapons prior to the test scenario, the wall would have been toast.

"See?" he said.

"I see," Torrance replied. "That's not good."

Kluvac broke in. "At this rate, waving at a friend will get you torched."

Torrance chuckled. "Very succinct, Lieutenant."

He looked at Ramista. Her face grew a shade darker with his glance. She was younger than Skiles, with a fresh face and widely spaced eyes.

"I read the daily brief on the issue this morning," Torrance said to her. "Have you already installed the latest movement algorithm patch on this system?" he asked.

"Yes," she replied.

"So that should be fine," Torrance mused. "Maybe a code problem? Something in the pattern recognition area?"

"That's what I thought at first, too," Skiles replied. He motioned toward Ramista. "But Angela's been over the source code and its module-level test reports twice. We fixed some autogen bugs in the software's original installation, and patched a problem with an error-state parameter, but nothing else seems out of order."

"What mission overlay are you using?"

"Base diplomatic," Skiles replied curtly.

That was good. The system could be programmed with several overlays—which were basically mission profiles that would give the captain the ability to call for different levels of sensitivity depending on how skittish he felt about the mission at any one time. The "base diplomatic" overlay was a slightly higher degree of sensitivity than "standard operations," and considerably less sensitive than "battle stations."

Torrance looked at Skiles and wondered about the sharpness of his tone. Few of *Orion*'s crew were pleased about the fundamentals of their next mission.

"Have we looked at the infrared input?" he said. "Maybe the fact that the feed doesn't have a human heat signature is confusing it."

"Just starting to look at that, but first blush says H-MADS resolved the test subject appropriately—human robot, unarmed, lots of other qualifiers."

A single beep came from the hallway comm port. "Captain's message for Commander Black," Abke said.

"I'll take it now," Torrance replied.

"The captain requests you report to the bridge, sir."

"Timing?"

"I infer immediacy."

"Thank you," Torrance said.

The computer went silent.

The team looked at him. The admiral would have his butt if H-

MADS was off-line for this mission. This was why he was here, after all. But he'd been in the trenches before. Troubleshooting took whatever time it took, and the only thing he could do was make sure the team was comfortable.

"Well, all right, then," Torrance said. "You know where we are. We've got a few days to deal with this, but I don't need to tell you that the big picture says we're way behind. I need this working last week. Do your best. I'll try to keep Douglas off your backs, all right?"

"Yes, sir," Skiles said.

"But I expect total focus until this is fixed, got it? And when it *is* fixed, I expect it will be right. You need me, you buzz. I'll drop anything I'm working on to see you get what you need."

"Aye, sir," Skiles said.

Torrance hoped his smile came off warmly. Then he turned and headed toward the bridge.

————

Torrance felt the pressure of attention the moment he stepped onto the bridge. Command station operators looked at him from the corners of their eyes, interested but self-conscious enough to avoid being caught staring. It was as if his presence projected a magnetic field, or as if a telepathic message had been sent across the room as soon as he appeared: *Hero on the floor*.

"Commander Black," Captain Douglas said. He stood in the doorway of his conference room. "Welcome to my bridge. Please come in."

"Thank you," Torrance replied.

Douglas was thirty-five years old—very young for a Star Drive captain. He stood six inches taller than Torrance and had a pair of thin, tapering hips that combined with strapping shoulders to give him the crisp aura of a hawkish kite. Dressed in a full dark work suit, the captain looked like a giant exclamation point.

His bio read like a laundry list of achievements. Summa cum laude at the Academy, impressive responsibility and equally impressive results at three stations leading to command of forward units running special ops. It was obvious Douglas had his mind set on greater things.

"Let's have a little discussion," the captain said, motioning toward his personal briefing room.

Torrance crossed the bridge and entered the room.

The austere nature of the office suggested the captain wasn't planning to stay long, accentuating Torrance's opinion that Douglas considered this position as a stepping stone. A work desk and control display sat to Torrance's right. The main meeting area was filled with a white oval table and several chairs.

"It's a different kind of ship, isn't it?" Douglas said, noting Torrance's curiosity as he stepped around the table.

"Yes, sir," Torrance said. "Everything's different."

And it was.

Everguard's briefing center had been large and spacious in order to accommodate representatives of all the systems needed to support several thousands of people. Star Drive ships didn't need to staff for sustainability over decades-long trips, so everything was smaller.

He picked his way to a seat.

The table included display systems embedded in plastiglass covers and spaced at a proper distance to support a comfortable seating pattern. A trio of ceiling-mounted projector units provided a three-dimensional map of the Eta Cass binary in the center space of the area. The G-type primary star held the prominent central position while the K3 secondary floated nearby.

Four blue points were shown outside the binary.

These were planets—Clotho, Atropos, and Lachesis, named after the three fates, orbited the primary, and Galopar orbited the secondary star of the pair. He thought of the fates: Clotho, who spun the thread of life; Lachesis, who dispensed and measured it; and Atropos, who cut the thread that consigned each soul's span.

Atropos was the center of attention, though.

Atropos was rich enough in titanium to make it a prime candidate for a manufacturing facility. And almost certainly it was for that reason that U3 had chosen to establish Atropos as their home planet.

"I need H-MADS operational tomorrow," the captain said as he settled into a chair.

The bluntness of the comment caught Torrance off stride. "Impossible," he replied.

"Systems people thrive on the impossible, eh, Commander?"

"Difficult is fun, yes," Torrance replied. "Impossible wrecks careers."

"Tomorrow. 0800 hours," the captain said in a firm tone.

"Sir, with all due respect. I've just come aboard and—"

"—and you want me to abort this mission because you're taking your time in getting up to speed? Is that what you want to go down in the record, Commander? You want history to record that the first UG diplomatic mission was hamstrung because a tired commander couldn't manage to get his new system running?"

"No, sir."

"Neither do I." The captain crossed his hands over his belly. "U3 has accepted our offer to discuss a settlement. The ambassador has cleared his calendar, so the mission has a new schedule. Tomorrow we're jumping to Universe Three's star system, Commander. Whether I agree with this mission or not, we're going to execute it. That means I intend to have a U3 delegation aboard soon, and I expect H-MADS to be fully operational to defend this ship's crew in case our guests have decided to do anything…untoward."

Torrance scratched his chin. "We're working on an interaction problem right now. It's an issue that causes exceptionally bad false positive assessment of aggression. And, to be honest, the interface to the weapons system has only been tested at the component level. So even if we can correct the problem, we're going to struggle to have a system we have any confidence with in the time frame you're asking."

"Then you'll fix it," the captain replied. "And you'll test it."

"Sir, this isn't really a matter of fixing anything so much as it's a matter of getting it to work right in the first place. The team is on it—I was troubleshooting the problem with them when you called, actually. I know I'm new here, but even I know this is a complex system with a history of being painful to operate. It doesn't take a scholar to predict that we'll find more things that need to be changed, even after the testing is complete."

"This is a job you were assigned to do, Commander. Don't tell me you can't do it."

The captain's gaze had an edge to it, a sharpness encrypted with underlying motives. This was a man who could go nova on command.

"I understand," Torrance said.

"So we launch tomorrow morning per schedule."

Torrance gritted his teeth. "I think that's a mistake, sir. But you're the CO. I'll follow your lead."

Douglas leaned forward, his fingers splayed over the desktop to support his weight. The smell of his cologne was sharp and arid.

"I don't care if you *are* a goddamned hero, Commander. This is not a test lab. This is a mission-ready Star Drive cruiser, and we are a day away from meeting a diplomatic crew from Universe Three—a group that's shown zero compunction to play by the rules. You've got the best WSO in the fleet, and you're the hottest shipboard systems man in the pipeline right now. So, no bullshit, Torrance. No coming back later and saying I told you so. Either you make this happen on schedule, or I file a performance report."

Silence grew between them. The star map hung in space to Torrance's left, Atropos gleaming blue.

"Aye, sir," he said. "I understand."

CHAPTER 6

Atropos, Eta Cassiopeia System
Local Date: Studna 23, 9
Local Time: 0540

Deidra's footsteps echoed off the walls as she stomped down the hallway. The space closed in on her. Heat rose to her face as the wave of overloud voices coming from the Exchange Room filled the hallway behind her. She pounded the meat of her fist against the doorway as she turned the corner into the stairwell. It raised a welt that she flexed away as she scampered down the stairs, through the door, and out into the fresh air.

Hot breeze whipped her hair across her face.

She shook it away and walked faster.

This decision was stupid. Anyone with sense could see that. This decision said that it was possible that the United Government and Universe Three could live in the same world—but that was wrong. Clearly wrong. The United Government would never leave them alone. Papa's condescension, saying that her reaction was about the fact that she was young, was wrong, too.

They were idiots. All of them. Even Papa.

This was their chance.

They were blowing their chance to live a life that could finally be guaranteed to be free of the Solar System and its oppressive oligarchy.

She growled out loud and strode through an open marketplace, ignoring men who hawked bread and meats, and shouldering past a young girl trying to trade blankets she had hand-stitched. Eta Cass was directly overhead and the only clouds were a smearing of gauzy-white on the horizon.

Deidra pressed her lips into a determined line as she left the marketplace behind and came to the edge of the wooded area nearby. As she passed between tree trunks, she thought about Katriana Martinez—the woman who had been mentoring her since their first days on the planet. Deidra's mother always said Deidra had to learn to bite back her responses and process them into something positive. Katriana's approach was similar, but different in the end. Even when she hadn't been in a position to do something about it, Katriana understood anger. Katriana Martinez had lost much in her life—her daughters, her father, and her mate—and she had been powerless to exact justice when those things happened. She understood when something was wrong, and she understood the relationship between vengeance and justice. She understood the value of time. She understood that being powerless did not mean there was nothing she could do.

This was what Deidra was thinking when she came to the lake and took a seat on her favorite rock.

She gave a long yell.

It helped.

She sat in the lakeside quiet while the sound of her voice faded into the distance.

"Want to tell me about it?"

The voice startled her so much she almost fell into the water.

Kel Melody was seated up in the nook of the tree she liked so much.

"Damn it, Kel. You scared the crap out of me."

"I figured I might find you here," she replied.

"Why's that?"

Kel swung out of the tree, landing with a lithe movement and coming to stand next to her.

"Just a lucky guess, I suppose," Kel replied. "I mean, who can say what it means when all the big dogs run off to an emergency meeting of the council? Maybe they just decided to get together to talk about the price of beans, right? I mean, who could possibly guess that my radical sweetie might leave that kind of a thing in a huff?"

Deidra smiled.

Kel was her age—six months older. Her mother was an agricultural specialist, working to match seeding to nutrients in the soil. Her father had been with a security detachment that was left on Io to make sure the UG wasn't able to trace their bugout. He hadn't made it back. Deidra and Kel had met at his award memorial, and gotten along together well enough to keep a running friendship. It was only years later that it had gotten complicated.

"Price of beans," Deidra said. "Funny."

Kel gave Deidra's shoulder a brief massage. "So, are prices going up or down?"

"Down," Deidra said. "Everything is going down."

Kel sat next to Deidra, using her butt to push her way onto the stone.

They sat together, looking over the water.

This was Deidra's favorite place.

She liked the sound of the water and the smell of the plants, specifically the purple reeds she called cattails even though they weren't close to the classic river weeds on Earth. Their roots were oval and colored with green at the base before fading toward that deep purple at the tips of their stalks. By the end of summer they grew heavy and bent, and then, over a period of a week or so, their pink and red flowers would burst and they would drop seeds into the brackish waters.

She liked that. The reeds working with the water to keep themselves alive. That was their purpose. Live. Expand over the shoreline. Drop their seeds for the next generation.

"So," Kel said. "What's happening?"

Deidra held her tongue. She wanted to say something, but she wasn't sure what. How do you decide to tell the person you share everything with that you can't share this?

"I don't know. But it's going to be bad."

"Talk to your father. Tell him what you think."

"He already knows."

"Maybe try again?" Kel said through a crooked smile. Her voice raised in that gentle wave she got when she was telling Deidra to calm down, but didn't want to say the words *calm down*. "This time without the yelling and screaming?"

Deidra laughed.

Kel was right, though. She had to talk to Papa again. Had to find a way to get him to see what a colossally bad idea this was. Didn't he read history? Didn't he understand what the UG was?

Deidra thought for a bit.

What would Katriana do? How would she respond to this thing her leadership was going to do?

A ring grew out in the middle of an alcove.

One of the water creatures that was half-fish, half-lizard, rising to feed on a water bug.

Maybe Papa was just getting old, she thought, senile, or maybe just growing soft as he aged. Maybe he was pretending he could make the UG into something it wasn't. Whatever. All she could say for sure was that while she and her Papa shared ideas about what Universe Three's perfect world would look like, they clearly disagreed with what it was going to take to achieve it.

She shrugged, and her shoulder rubbed against Kel's.

"Yes," she finally said. "I've got to try again."

———

An hour later, Deidra ignored privacy protocol and stepped directly into her father's office. Since he was old-school and hadn't allowed an automatic controller to be installed on the entryway, the door slammed against the wall as she burst in.

"I cannot believe we're going to do this," she said without hesitation.

She had to sidestep to keep from getting hit as the door swung back at her. The day hadn't gotten any cooler, and the thirty-minute power-walk she had taken to gather her thoughts had resulted in a line of sweat that rode on top of her forehead. Her face was flush with exertion.

The office was cluttered.

Papa sat on a couch in the corner, holding his arm out for Dr. Iwal as the physician reseated a C-Pak band around the upper half of his biceps. Gregor Anderson stood across the room, his arms clasped behind his back and his head down as if in contemplation.

A projection display of the Eta Cass system hovered on one side of the low table between them, and a layout of what she recognized as Atropos City's growth plan was sitting on the other side of the table.

"Are you all right?" Deidra said.

"Yes," Papa said. "I am fine."

He glanced at Dr. Iwal to dismiss him.

"Leave it on for the next three hours," Iwal said, standing up and shaking his head as he picked up a scanning device. He gathered up scraps of sterile paper that until a few minutes ago had been a packet storing an antibiotic pad. "And—I don't care if you feel like you're superhuman or not—fifteen minutes with the compression jacket every day."

Casmir Francis, leader of Universe Three, grumbled.

Gregor cleared his throat as the doctor picked his way past Deidra and closed the door behind him.

The time it took for the doctor to leave was long enough that the rawness of her anxiety began to creep back. On the other hand, it also allowed her to catch her breath.

Papa donned the shirt that had been laid over the back of the couch. "It's time to try a different path," Papa said, already beginning to explain himself as he rolled the shirt sleeve over the C-Pak.

"It's time to take control is what it is," Deidra replied.

"That is not what the gathering said."

"I heard them. But we both know it didn't have to be that way. Or that it doesn't have to be that way. Even now. You've turned them to your side before."

Papa patted the seat next to him. "Come and sit, my fervent daughter."

"I'll stand, thank you."

He let out one of those blustery sighs Deidra had come to hate. Her father could be an ass sometimes.

"It's not too late, Papa," she said. "This is the moment we've been waiting for. We can change the plan."

Papa sat back on the couch, resigned to be alone there.

"You're right, Deidra. This is the moment we've been waiting for. It's the moment when we arrange for our own sovereignty. It's the moment when we can begin to develop the agreements that will allow us to live free of the specter of the United Government."

"Not if it's a trap."

"The UG would not risk *Orion* if it wasn't dire for them. I think it's time to take that chance."

Deidra put her hands on her hips but didn't say anything.

Despite his earlier stonewalling, she had hoped her father was on her side, that he had merely been swayed to take a different path than he would have otherwise. But here he sat, with his most pedantic expression and a holier-than-thou attitude flowing out of his pores like it was some kind of invisible cloud.

"I can't believe this," she finally said.

Anderson came to stand behind a side chair between them, and gestured to the map of the Eta Cass system. He was older than Papa, and his hands showed it. "We aren't blind to the idea that it could be a trap, Deidra," he said. "We're working out the mechanics of a defense and retaliation plan now."

She looked closely at the display.

A representation of *Orion* sat at coordinates in orbit above Galopar, the plot of land the UG had used to create the secret base they had launched their original attack on Atropos City from many years ago.

Two ships hung nearby the outpost, *Einstein* posted between *Orion* and Atropos, and *Icarus*, posted on the opposite side of Galopar. From that position, *Icarus* would be able to use the planet to edge out of direct line of sight with only a moment's notice. Data readouts showed both ships' weapons were trained on *Orion*.

Strings of smaller vessels were laid on a line parallel to both U3 ships—skimmers and jumpers that Deidra didn't need a military education to see would have made the trip to the rendezvous point in the bays of the Excelsior craft. Their weapons were smaller than *Einstein*'s or *Icarus*'s, but they were also trained on the UG craft, creating a crosshatched killing field of sorts.

She glanced to Papa.

"We will destroy *Orion* if they take any action against our negotiating party," he said. "We will find a way to broadcast that to them in advance. And if there is one thing we both know, it is that losing *Orion* will be unacceptable to the United Government, even if they were able to destroy one of ours in the process. They cannot manage if we have a Star Drive craft and they do not."

Deidra couldn't argue that.

Any game of pure attrition would leave the United Government without interstellar jump capability, and Universe Three with a free rein to hit any base or outpost that the UG might have.

"What if they attack both our ships at once?"

"That's what the skimmer lines are for," Anderson replied.

She chewed her bottom lip. "What if they are okay with two-for-one?"

"That's the right question. They will need to know we're ahead of them in our ability to produce another Star Drive. As long as they understand we will have a period of time when we can ride the stars and they cannot, we should be safe."

Deidra scanned the flashing model. "I still don't like it," she said.

"Good," Anderson responded, the tone of his voice carrying a strong undercurrent.

"Why do you say it that way?"

Anderson pursed his lips and glanced at Papa.

The twist of Papa's eyebrow was affirmative.

"I want you to be part of the implementation team," Anderson said.

"When your father and I are finished here, I want to meet with you to discuss the details of our plans. Specifically, I want you to lead communication and training of the weapons commanders of each ship."

Deidra brought her brows together.

"You're promoting me?"

"You've been in navigation," Papa said, smiling. "And you've participated in the planning of the city. You have managed several smaller ops." He pointed to the display of Eta Cass and her planetary system. "We've even had you sit in on some of the conversations about how to expand our population across the system as we gain more access to Star Drive systems."

"What are you saying?"

"It's time for us to be clear that you are preparing to take command of Universe Three," he replied. "You're very young. The fact that you reacted so quickly to this situation shows you're not ready, yet. But it's also clear to everyone by now that you're the right person to become my successor. You've got the drive. You've got the background. It's time that you step into a bigger role now. When this action is finished, I'm going to want you to become Gregor's assistant."

Discord between being upset at the tactics Papa was proposing, and the thrill of hearing that she was actively proposed as the future leader of Universe Three pulled at her.

"As it stands now," Papa said, "Gregor will lead in the interim if anything untoward happens to me, but he is not of the right generation to lead us across the universe. You are. Being his assistant will give you access to everything we do."

"I see."

A grin fought to come to her face, but Deidra pushed it back and turned to Anderson.

"Where should we meet?" she said.

He rubbed his fingertips over the wood of the chair back he had been leaning on. "Your quarters would be fine. Or anywhere else, really. Just leave word."

"All right," she said, realizing that the two men wanted privacy now.

Deidra opened the door, left the room, and closed it behind her. She leaned her head back against the hard surface. Only then did she allow herself to break out in an expression of full-fledged joy.

CHAPTER 7

UGIS *Orion*
Local Date: January 24, 2215
Local Time: 0845

f Torrance knew anything right now, it was that he had to find a way to bring Commander Yuan into the team. He found her leaning over a table at Weapons Command.

A gathering of ensigns surrounded her as she pointed to targeting zones on the datascreen. "It's all a big game of 3-D tag," she said to the gathering. "But inertia is a bitch, and you just can't get around good old Newton at serious subluminal."

The gathering gave a polite chuckle.

"May I have a word with you, Commander?" Torrance said.

The room grew an awkward silence.

Yuan straightened and met Torrance's gaze. She was short and thin, her dark hair styled off her face. Her rounded eyes were brown flecked with gray, her skin smooth over high cheekbones. Her lips had been painted on in what was outdated, but understated perfection. From her arched eyebrows to the crease in her trousers, her entire being radiated precision.

"Can it wait, sir?" she replied with an expression that said she was busy.

"No, I'm afraid it can't."

She shut off the display with a deliberate motion, then walked away from the gathering with a gait that gave a message somewhere between direct confrontation and submission to his stature as her commanding officer.

"Have you come up with any ideas as to what might be causing our H-MADS difficulties?" Torrance said when they were away from earshot of her weapons team.

"I would appreciate if, in the future, you would call me out of this type of session in a less embarrassing fashion."

"Pardon me?"

"You've shown my team that I am subordinate to you. It erodes my credibility."

Torrance considered several responses.

"I apologize if you feel that way, Commander," he said, hoping to at least deflect any direct confrontation. "But this is important."

"No, sir. I don't have any ideas about how to fix your H-MADS issue—but, then, that's not really my problem, is it?"

"H-MADS is a weapon system," Torrance stated.

"With all due respect, sir, the weapons component of that shipboard system checks out fine. The laser's targeting algorithm is accurate to within ten-thousandths of a degree, and the firing mechanism has proven one hundred percent reliable."

"You and I both know that interface issues can be caused by either side of any system, and therefore can be fixed in the same fashion."

"My laser interfaces just fine with every other firing assembly on the ship."

"I don't care about that."

"Since you are *Orion*'s Systems *and* Weapons commander," Yuan said, "perhaps you should."

She stared at him like a prideful cat. He had never commanded someone so overtly insubordinate.

"I'm not going to argue with you, LiJuan."

She remained transfixed.

"A moment ago I was informed that we will jump tomorrow morning. That means we have until then to get this thing under control. You will work with the H-MADS team to fix this problem. If they go down, you go down. We *all* go down. Is that clear?"

"Clear as vacuum, sir."

"Good."

They stood together for several seconds, Torrance waiting for Yuan to break off, Yuan standing with defiance in her gaze.

"You are dismissed, Commander," Torrance finally said.

"Thank you, sir."

Yuan pivoted and returned to the gathering of technicians.

———

Still upset with the confrontation, Torrance stepped into his office and threw himself into his chair.

Damn it!

There was too much to do, too much to adjust to.

His team was new. Douglas was looming over him like a vulture, and Yuan was, well, Yuan was Yuan. The mission would launch tomorrow, and that in itself meant he had a thousand things to deal with outside of fixing this singular problem. Somehow, for example, he had to complete the full prelaunch shakedown in the free time he had between bouts of attempting to get H-MADS running.

He gripped the armrests hard enough that his fingers hurt. He hadn't been aboard long enough to clutter the desktop, so the system monitor stood out against the starkness of the flat surface. The carpet was a dark green synthetic that still had its plastic smell of newness.

"May I order something from the mess, sir?" the computer asked.

"No thanks, Abke."

He glanced at the clock and scratched the back of his neck. Past noon. Now that he had told Abke not to get him anything, he realized his stomach was empty.

A knock came at the door.

"Enter," Torrance said. The door clicked open, and footsteps rustled against the carpet.

"Do you have a moment?"

Torrance looked up to see Landis Marin, a group leader for the ship's atmospheric control team. She was nearly as tall as Torrance, and wore a pair of standard-issue blue workday pants and a collarless white shirt opened a single button at the neckline. Her hair was blond, cut in a short buzz that accentuated the startling edges of her Germanic features. Her shirt was marked with *Orion*'s insignia on the left shoulder, and the double crimson-rimmed stripes that noted her rank.

"I always have a moment, Lieutenant. Come on in. Have a seat."

She took a step further, then folded herself into the chair beside the desk. Her demeanor suggested she was being cautious, which made sense to Torrance. He was a new CO for her. Apprehension was always wise.

"What's the problem?"

"We can't get the air system balanced," Marin said. Her arms wrapped around themselves so that her hands cupped her elbows as she spoke. "The environmental processor is pulling from the starboard oxygen tanks but not from the port."

"Suggested action?"

"Take the port system off-line."

"And?"

"Flush the line to see if we've got obstruction in the filters or the antibacterial systems. Assuming nothing's there, then we start with the regulator system and work our way backwards until we find out what's wrong."

Torrance nodded.

Marin's performance reports indicated she was bright and very good at what she did. Structured in her approach to issues, and diligent to the point of annoyance to those who were not so driven toward perfection. But reading reports and seeing someone firsthand are two different things. This first face-to-face with her told him Landis Marin was as good as reported. She had an embryonic sense of confidence that rode just under a fragile shell of awkward discomfort.

"You're on the right track. Go ahead and follow that approach and see if it works."

"Thank you, sir. I will." Marin rose from the chair and turned toward the door.

"Landis?"

She paused in the doorway.

"Things are not going well on the H-MADS integration, and the captain is very interested in seeing that system working prior to launch."

"I can imagine that."

"It's also going to be announced shortly that the mission has been moved up."

"Moved up?"

"We're going to jump tomorrow."

Her eyes got wide and her eyebrows arched.

"So you see why I need to focus my energy on that effort."

"Yes, sir."

"Yet we still have to complete the prelaunch shakedown of the service and support systems."

"They're almost finished anyway, sir."

"That's true. But being almost finished and being finished are two very different things—as you see with this issue with the O2 balance, right?"

Marin pursed her thin lips.

Realizing she had taken his example as a reprimand, Torrance raised a hand.

"That's all right, Lieutenant. I didn't mean that as an accusation. I think you're doing a fantastic job."

"Thank you, sir."

"In fact," Torrance said. "If you feel you're up to it, I would like to give you authority to complete the shakedown yourself. I'll review your work, of course. And I'll be at your call if you need me. But your paperwork tells me your work is excellent, and you've already proven to me that you know what you're doing. I trust you'll do a great job."

Her face flushed with the compliment. "Thank you, sir. You can count on me."

Torrance contained a grin. "Good. I'll make the authorization."

Marin smiled.

"In the meantime—" He looked at the clock again. "—how about I get the system to send us some lunch, and you can tell me how you intend to complete the shakedown?"

Marin hesitated. "Well, uh. I've already eaten."

"Oh."

"And if I'm going to finish the shakedown anytime soon, I've got a lot of work to do."

"I understand completely." Torrance forced a smile. He always enjoyed how people's assessment of work changed when they were responsible for it. "I still want to see your plan, though."

"I can get it to you by 1400."

"That would be fine," he said.

Marin smoothed invisible wrinkles on the sides of her pants legs. "Thank you, sir."

The door shut behind her.

"Can I get you anything from the mess, sir?" Abke asked again.

"A sandwich, please. Egg salad with lettuce," he replied. "And something on the side to snack on."

"It will be here in a moment, sir."

Torrance sighed, and pulled up the system schedule. He had a problem to solve, with a brand-new crew and a critical team member who didn't like him. Launch was less than twenty-four hours away. Even after delegating the shakedown, this was going to take some doing.

CHAPTER 8

Atropos, Eta Cassiopeia System
Local Date: Studna 25, 9
Local Time: 1415

The low rumble of an approaching skimmer came from the distance.

Todias Nimchura stood and wiped sweat from his brow. He couldn't help but look at it as it drew near.

It was an old hovercraft, caked with layers of dust and dirt that would probably never fully come off without an acidic power wash. Its engines were probably out of date, too—pretty much like everything here. It would be a sluggish piece of shit to handle. Barely able to turn, and probably so slow it couldn't outrun half the animals on the planet. But it flew.

Just the thought of controlling it made his hands itch.

It was only Nimchura's God-given skills with a joystick that got him into Interstellar Command to begin with.

The skimmer drew to a stop maybe fifty meters away.

The pilot sat still as the passenger got out and discussed something with the shift leader. They referenced a datapad, then the shift leader pointed to Nimchura. The passenger looked his way, then nodded. The judgmental expressions on their faces made the hair on the back of his neck do cartwheels, and he was suddenly hyperaware of the grit he was grinding between his teeth. For a moment he considered walking over to them. He saw himself grabbing the pilot and throwing him out of the cockpit, felt the power of cramming the engine controller to get the thing spun up, and the pure joy of wrenching the skimmer away.

In that moment, Nimchura actually felt the ground fade, and the sense of gravity shift as the skimmer would slide away. He heard the whine of the power system, felt the shake of the seat below him.

Then he was back standing in the heat of the day, watching as his shift leader and the passenger confirmed something else, then watching the new arrival get back into the skimmer, listening as the engine rumbled to life again and the craft returned to wherever it originated from.

The shift leader glanced his way, and pointed at the flooring Nimchura had been working on.

"That's not gonna get done by itself, Flyboy," she called at him.

He pressed his lips together, then spit on the ground.

Asshole that the shift leader was, *Flyboy* had become her favorite name for him once she had come to realize what the idea of flying meant to him.

He glanced at the skimmer as it disappeared into a cloud of brown dust.

Strange, Nimchura thought.

He had never been the focus of a visit before.

He returned to his pour.

———

It was nearly dark when Nimchura stepped into his hut and slammed the door closed. The frame was out of alignment again. He had to twist it around to get everything to fit together. When he held it just right, the thing closed with a grating sound of wood on concrete that just served to piss him off even more. That's how it was here. Always something wrong. Always something to fix.

"You're later than usual," Hadri said, sitting on the mattress they had pushed up against the far wall. A personal reader glowed on her lap. She looked at him through dark eyes that were made darker by the hut's lack of reasonable lighting.

"Sorry," he said. "I think they moved the schedule up."

They had been together three years now. She had been good for him. It was a relationship Nimchura had fought, but Hadri, he had learned over time, was a woman who knew how to get what she wanted.

Nimchura declined her advances at first because, even though U3's leadership had set him free a year before, he was still busy playing the part of wronged captive. His behavior during two years of lockup had proven he wasn't particularly aligned to the UG, but he wasn't aggressive or obnoxious, and it became more of a pain in the ass to take care of him than let him go, so he was a free man, now. As free as anyone else, anyway.

Later he rebuffed Hadri because he thought she was just looking for something unusual and he didn't want to be anyone's pet. Hadri Kamila was an academic in the ranks of free citizens, a woman who worked in anthropology and social structures. He assumed she wanted him so she could dangle him in front of her friends as much as anything else. Despite the fact that he found her to be attractive, he had wanted to be alone. So, it had taken time.

Thank the powers she was also persistent.

Of course, it turned out that Hadri *had* wanted him as much for the aura of forbidden fruit that surrounded him in those early days as anything else. Her job may have been about social norms, but her interests ran toward the unique and unusual, in more ways than one. There were few people more unique or unusual back then than Todias Nimchura, a shot-down UG pilot from Tupelo, Mississippi. In the end, it had worked, though. He liked her independence, she liked cracking his personality—or at least the fact that he hid it so well.

Nimchura sat next to her and put his head back against the wall. Hadri rubbed his arm.

Their hut was tiny but not unusual for the city, five meters to a side, with a concrete floor he had been given permission to pour himself, a permission he understood even then was given more as a way to prove Universe Three was willing to play ball than for any particular fairness. They framed the walls with wood from trees that grew in the forest a half mile away. Gaps in the cracks were filled with a gummy pitch that often needed replacement. The roof was a mix of water-retaining bark he had peeled from trees, and thatched reeds he had pulled from downstream on the lake and riverbed that flowed out beyond the city. The two of them decorated it with a rotating array of art and other knickknacks that struck their fancy. Today, he saw Hadri had brought in a tangled branch of the white-barked tree that grew so prevalently in the area.

It was interesting, he thought. Twisted in a hundred different directions. Fitting for her. He understood why she liked it.

"I waited to cook," she said, not mentioning the fact that it was his turn.

"That's good."

"Long day, I guess."

The rough surface of the wall rubbed against his head as he nodded. He pressed his skull harder into the wall to quell a small headache. His shoulders and arms were numb with fatigue. The specter of the skimmer weighed on him. He wanted to fly. It was all he could think of—that sense of being on or in a piece of machinery that was gliding on thin air, or rolling out in deep space. He wanted to feel the thrust of engines, hear the sounds of a plane or a jumper as it made its flight. For a minute he wanted to talk about it, but he looked at Hadri and knew she couldn't understand.

This, he thought, was the thing he missed the most about the service—missed the most about Deuce Jarboe, his wing leader who had died during the attack UG made on the city.

"Let me get to cooking, then."

Hadri set the reader aside, and rolled to her knees before taking one lurching step toward the open pit in the far corner. She pulled herself up on a small stool as she plugged a cord in that led to the ventilation fan they had mounted on the wall above the recess. The fan kicked on with a grating hum, and ensured errant smoke was evacuated. She lit a fire with a gas wand, turned up the wick, and put a pair of packets on the grate that lay above the flames. The packets were a mix of meat and vegetables, wrapped in a sheath of what was essentially a ground corn tortilla shell. She also put a kettle of pasta and water on the grate.

The aroma of cooking meat and boiling noodles filled the room.

Nimchura closed his eyes and kept his head tilted back.

It felt like rain might come this evening. It had rained earlier in the day, and the thatch still smelled damp.

Hadri returned, planting a kiss on Nimchura's lips.

"How did your day go?" Nimchura said, not opening his eyes.

"It was good," she replied.

A pounding came at the door.

"Todias Nimchura?" a voice called.

Hadri's expression clouded.

"What is it?" Nimchura yelled, raising to one knee.

"Please open the door, sir."

He glanced around the hut, suddenly feeling its lack of size with more intensity than he had before. He stood, grabbed another stool by one leg, and, holding it as a weapon, opened the door.

By the light of their fire, he saw it was a U3 security officer. A young man with a detachment of three more support staff behind him.

"What is it?"

"I need you to come with me, sir."

"We're just getting ready to eat."

Nimchura relaxed his arm with the stool, but did not drop it.

"I'm sure the director will ensure you get a meal, sir."

"The director?"

Nimchura frowned. What could Casmir Francis want with him? In the distance of his mind he recalled the passenger of the skimmer and the way his shift boss looked at him as she pointed Nimchura's way.

"Is this about the skimmer?"

"I couldn't say, sir. I just need you to come with me."

Nimchura looked at Hadri.

She shrugged. "Go," she said.

"All right."

He went to put the stool down, but the memory of the work site and the skimmer came over him like a wave of heat. He felt his shift leader point at him, and the man turn to gaze at him with such… contempt. In that moment the hair on his neck rose again, and he felt… caged—remembering the skimmer, and feeling the ground pressing up through his feet.

He left his body then.

Or at least that's how he would remember it.

He straightened himself, still holding the stool by one awkward leg, still wearing his work clothes. "Can I clean up?" he said.

"No, sir. My orders are to bring you directly."

"I see," Nimchura replied.

And he swung the stool, feeling the weight of the wood turn in his hand, catching the stooge in the face and the shoulder with the looping arc of the blow. The man fell with a grunt. Nimchura was already spinning on one leg and grabbing the stool by two legs to bring it crashing down on a second guard.

The smell of blood came to him.

It felt good.

Familiar in an odd way.

He thought of flying. Slicing through clouds and into open air, racing through a field of debris, turning the spacecraft and heading in a dive straight toward ground that was rushing up at him with blinding speed.

Which is where he found himself.

On the dry dirt outside the hut, cheek digging into the grit and the fire of something ringing at the top of his head, something too sharp to be identified at first, but was going to grow into a wave of red hot pain right about…now.

He tried to raise up, but the last thing he saw was the boot of the third guard swinging toward his face.

Then it got dark.

CHAPTER 9

UGIS *Orion*
Local Date: January 25, 2215
Local Time: 0115

Torrance sat slouched in a chair beside the briefing podium. The rest of the systems team was scattered about *Orion*'s auditorium room, filling about a quarter of its fifty seats. The air was stuffy and tense. It reminded him a lot of a night spent on *Everguard* several years back.

"I don't know what else to do," Skiles said, leaning back in his padded seat and staring at the ceiling. After an eighteen-hour shift, Skiles looked as tired as Torrance felt. His uniform jacket was unzipped to the sternum, his eyes were faded and bleary, and his longish hair was frayed from having had a hand run through it far too many times. A light shadow of stubble was forming on his chin. "We've been through every piece of code in the optical sensor, and hand-checked every pattern the recognition system is based on," he said.

"There's nothing there, Commander," Ramista added from the seat beside Skiles.

The two were an item, Torrance realized that now. They hadn't told anyone, yet, but he could see it in the way they worked together, the way their eyes locked at certain moments and how they gave each other a comfortable space to work in.

"What's the latest on the optics package?" Torrance asked.

Kluvac replied from the front row. "It's clean, sir. We swapped out all three subassemblies, and they tested fine."

"Weapons?"

All heads turned to Commander Yuan, who sat calmly by herself on the left side of the auditorium.

"The weapons systems all test fine."

"Are you certain?"

Yuan toggled a controller and pointed the infrared port to the holo projector. "I can walk you through the checkout procedure if you would like, sir." She held her finger over the button that would transfer data to the projector, and stared at him with ice-cold intensity. Her hair and makeup were still perfectly in place despite the hour. Her movements were still precise.

Torrance fought to control himself. He didn't need this.

"No, Commander," he said. "Thank you, anyway. No reason to drag the team through it at this time of the morning. I'll look at your procedures later."

He scanned the auditorium. The team's eyes all shifted under his gaze, glancing sideways or down at their feet. He was Torrance Black, hero. Or maybe he was just Torrance Black, their latest command flunky. Regardless, they were worried, and they didn't know how to relate to him. Worse—they were watching him, judging him, seeing how he handled himself, and trying to assess who he was. He realized then how valuable Karl Malloy's sense of humor had been.

Just the thought gave him an angry chill.

Torrance stood and strolled across the stage, his chin in his hand. He spoke in a train of thought as he walked. "Well," he said. "That's it, then. The captain has made it clear he intends to launch at 0800 regardless of whether this system is working or not."

He paused and looked at Skiles.

"Do you think I have a chance at the record for the shortest command of all time?"

Skiles, caught off guard, squirmed in his chair.

Ramista grinned, though, and a few others chuckled. The rest laughed when Torrance followed with his best try at mimicking Malloy's boyish grin while giving what he hoped was a comic shrug.

"That's better," he said. "We've got to lighten up. We've got to expand our minds here. If the obvious isn't working, then we've got to think differently and find something else."

A familiar voice came from the back of the room.

"What if you mask it, sir?"

Torrance looked up to see Thomas Kitchell at the top of the auditorium's stairway.

The young man was standing straight, though it was clear his posture was coming at a cost. He wore an Academy blue shirt over his dark pants, and a dark jacket over the shirt. The sleeve that peeked from under the coat carried the *Everguard* patch and a set of three citations.

"Thomas," Torrance said, suddenly unable to utter a different word.

Kitchell came down the stairs, holding onto the rail with each step. "I said, what if you mask it?"

"What do you mean?" Skiles said.

Kitchell got to the bottom of the stairs and steadied himself.

"I've seen all the specs and some of the failure reports. The system is interpreting hand and arm adductions as an aggressive maneuver, and somehow triggering the firing command, right? So, if we can't figure out what's wrong, maybe the best thing would be just to remove that trigger altogether. If nothing else, you've still got a ninety-five percent system, which is better than the nothing you'll have if you shut it all down."

The auditorium was silent as the idea settled in.

"It was just a thought," Kitchell murmured.

"And it was a good one," Torrance said. "Just what we needed."

"Who is this?" Yuan said. She was sitting forward now.

Torrance went to the young man and took his hand. Kitchell's grip was firm and warm. He put his arm around the boy, who wasn't so much a boy anymore, and clasped him into a tight hug. When they parted, Torrance took him in from close up, hands on both shoulders, seeing Kitchell's tired face and his worn posture but also feeling the power of the kid's presence. Torrance was torn by the need to laugh and cry at the same time.

"From the looks of it," Torrance finally said, "I would say this is Academy Ensign Thomas Kitchell."

Then he turned to the rest of the crew.

"Let me introduce you to the real hero of *Everguard*."

An awkward moment of silence came over the room.

"Just one of the heroes," Kitchell muttered.

"Thomas worked under me on *Everguard*," Torrance said. "He's a bright guy. Very soon the two of us are going to spend some serious time talking about how he happened to arrive here at this moment, but right now I'm declaring him part of the team. Have a seat, Thomas."

Kitchell gave a tired grin, then took the nearest seat.

The rest of the team was still adjusting to his presence and to the masking idea he had just flopped onto the table in front of them, but they hadn't rejected him and a few were throwing him sideways glances, clearly trying to assess what his appearance meant.

"Any other ideas?" Torrance asked.

"We could call off the mission!"

"Great!" he quipped. "I'll get the captain on the line and you can give him that idea personally."

The auditorium broke out in smiles.

"What if we shut down the hallway system, and utilize H-MADS only in the conference center?"

"That's probably the safest thing," Skiles said. "But will it fly with upper command?"

"I don't know," Torrance said, turning to stand before Commander Yuan. "Would you pitch it with me, LiJuan?"

Yuan nodded absently.

"I don't know that it's necessary, though. If the software mask your friend suggested works, it should be equally safe everywhere. But shutting down hallway coverage might be a good political move."

"You mean it might cost me that record for shortest command?"

Even Yuan's lips curled into a tiny smile at that. "Yes, Commander. It might cost you that record."

"Great," he said. "Then that's it. Let's mask the infringing activity. I want a report as soon as it's done, and I want a test sequence completed as quickly as possible thereafter. The captain's prelaunch brief is at 0700, so Commander Yuan and I will meet at 0600 to go over the test data and prepare our recommendation." He looked at Yuan.

She nodded.

"Okay, then. Let's get to it."

The group broke up to the sound of invigorated conversation and hasty footsteps.

Torrance looked at Kitchell. "Do you have a minute?"

Kitchell gave a sheepish grin. "Can it wait? I want to watch the masking."

A huge smile broke over Torrance's face. "That's so like you."

"I learned from the best."

"Go to it, then. But you're not getting out of here without talking to me."

"Wouldn't think of it, LC."

Torrance gave a double take.

"I know you've been promoted, sir, but if it's edge with you, you'll always be LC to me," Kitchell said as he got up to follow Skiles and Ramista. "Best rank ever."

"Fair enough," Torrance said.

He watched as Kitchell carefully traversed the steps up. After the kid made it to the top and slipped out of the room, Torrance drew a deep breath and rubbed fatigue out of his eyes. He hoped this was going to work.

"Hey," he said as he stood alone in the auditorium. "Take a chance, right?"

Then he picked his hat off the podium, and followed the path Kitchell had taken.

CHAPTER 10

Atropos, Eta Cassiopeia System
Local Date: Conejo 3, 9
Local Time: 1215

After going over the operation with the entire group, Deidra briefed each skimmer pilot individually, walking through their positions on the line and the coordinates their energy weapons would cover. *Einstein*'s skimmers would lay a line between the UG ship and Atropos. *Icarus*'s skimmers would form up in a wall that used Galopar itself as the zero-point to intersect with *Einstein*'s skimmers. Each Z-pad was equipped with a single plasma cannon that had been modified with centrifugal recyclers to boost its projectile's velocity.

Six were to focus on *Orion*'s Star Drive unit.

Two each on her impulse power systems.

The rest had individual targets.

Einstein would cover *Orion*'s weaponry and her mag-shields. *Icarus* would focus on the bridge itself.

The plan was well designed.

Still, Deidra was worried.

Despite Papa's certainty, and despite Gregor Anderson's suggestion that accepting UG diplomacy was the best answer, she was leaving no stone unturned, no situation uncovered. If the Uglies tried anything at all, they would pay. And deep in her heart, she still felt that she was right. The problem was that she was just one person. Beyond that, she wasn't stupid. She heard what people said—she understood they saw her as young and out of control, probably too emotional. If she stood up to her father now and she turned out to be wrong, there could be serious penalties to pay, and even though some didn't think so, Deidra understood exactly how and where political lines got drawn. She had studied Ellyn Parker, her father, and the entire history of disobedience. She understood that power was a game as much as it was a passion.

Life was long, she thought as she considered her options.

The op would run tomorrow, and weapons control was her area. She wasn't going to let anything go wrong.

———

It was well past midnight before Deidra arrived home. She was still anxious. Keyed up. She knew she had done her job, but in the end she couldn't help but feel an oppressive sense of gloom that covered her skin like an invisible layer of paste.

Kel was in the bedroom sleeping, but Jamal was still awake, listening to music on his buds. "Have some?" he said, raising a glass of the wine he fermented from the red fruit that grew wild on this planet. The liquid was deep and dark.

She took the glass, sipped, then gave it back.

The sharp spice filled the back of her throat. It was almost like cinnamon, one of her favorites.

"It's a good batch," she said.

"You're late again."

"Yeah," she said, her voice far away.

"You okay?"

She sat on the beanbag sack of a chair beside him.

When your father is the leader of the Free World, it's hard to know who to trust, but Deidra had been with Kel and Jamal for a year now. One of the reasons she stayed was that neither of them ever pressed her on anything. They knew who she was. They knew she couldn't share everything that happened to her, at least not right away. Jamal and Kel gave her space and accepted her for who she was, and neither had ever asked her for favors based on her position, and that meant everything to her.

Jamal ran a hand over her thigh, using the strength of his fingers to massage deep toward the bone. It felt marvelous. She couldn't help but groan.

Unlike Matt Anderson, Jamal was her kind of man.

He was darker and thinner than Anderson, but just as fun to look at. And he was just as dedicated to the more passionate ideals of U3 that Deidra carried around within her. But he was smarter than Anderson, and saw things from a much broader background. Where Matt Anderson was binary in his approach, Jamal understood angles. Anderson would always be capable, but there was little doubt that he would rise to whatever level he achieved as much because his father was Papa's second in command. Jamal was destined to find his own level, and despite his more laid-back presence Deidra was betting that Jamal would outdo Matt Anderson in the end. He was studying chemical engineering, with a bent toward biological systems and probably medicine. He wanted to cure the world of diseases, but right now he would probably settle for merely getting rid of the allergies that plagued him here on Atropos.

Besides being both fun and potent, the wine was a form of self-medication on that front—inducing local material from the flowering plants into his system seemed to control the breakouts.

Jamal understood people, and read situations. His quiet personality played off Deidra's fiery nature. Adding Kel's artistic bent to the balance gave them a stability Deidra enjoyed more than she had ever really considered before.

"I'm okay," she finally answered his question. But her voice betrayed a different truth.

Jamal put the glass down, then sat up to put his arm around her, rubbing her back. "Need anything?" The wide-eyed expression on his face made his implication clear. The aroma of his presence seemed to well up inside her. Yes, she thought. It would be nice to get lost in him right now.

She put her hand on his knee as he kissed her.

The fresh spice of wine on his lips made her breathe him in.

She put her other hand to the back of his head, and kissed him back.

"Is this an open party?"

They both turned to find Kel leaning against the doorway to the bedroom, a smile on her lips.

Deidra took in the languid form of her girlfriend draped in her gauzy wrap. The plans were set. What was going to happen was going to happen.

It would be good to let the world around her go on its own way.

If only for one evening.

CHAPTER 11

UGIS *Orion*
Local Date: January 25, 2215
Local Time: 0430

The time was beyond late, and Torrance was tired. The team had successfully tested the software mask. It seemed to work fine. Thank God. He hadn't slept, but he was too keyed up now, and *Orion* would depart in about three hours. It was clear he wasn't getting any shut-eye tonight.

He pulled up a report from Landis Marin that said the preflight testing was completed. Two small issues, both dealt with.

"LC?"

Torrance looked up to find Kitchell at his office door. He broke out in the biggest smile he had ever felt. He needed that.

"Thomas," he said, standing. He stepped around his desk, then leaned back, sitting with his butt on the desktop and his arms crossed.

Kitchell stepped in. "Hope I'm not interrupting. I wanted to stop by and say hey before you launch. Not sure if I was going to be able to see you again if I didn't."

"Of course it's not a problem. I would have personally kicked your behind if you didn't."

"I'm shipping out to the Academy tomorrow," Kitchell said.

"You'll be great."

"Yeah. I will."

Torrance chuckled. "Same old Thomas Kitchell, I see."

"I don't see getting shot as any reason to be otherwise, sir."

"I guess not."

"I thought you should know I'm planning on going Sig Ops."

Torrance paused. "Signal Ops?"

"Yes, sir. With a linguistics second."

"I see." And he did. Thomas Kitchell was going to focus on the data files. "Linguistics, too?"

"I don't know enough to play with the data you took, but it's gnawing at me. I want to know what they say, and assuming you're right, I figure we'll need people who can handle both sides of the fence."

"Risky."

Kitchell shrugged. "Take a chance, right?"

Torrance cocked his head and grinned. "I've heard that's an idea."

"Anyway. I got to skedaddle if I'm going to make the Academy shuttle."

Torrance stood up straight and shook Kitchell's hand, then broke down and gave the kid a hug. "Study well," Torrance said as they broke. "And call me if you learn anything."

"You too, all right?" The young man's gaze held a deeper question.

"Fair enough," Torrance replied. "I'm not giving up on them either. Maybe we can work together again."

"That would be great, LC. Totally great."

"Edge?" Torrance said.

"Edge as hell, sir."

Kitchell left, then, and Torrance returned to his seat, feeling better than he had felt since well before the whole *Everguard* mission jumped the shark. He looked at his system clock, and saw the security team's notice that said Ambassador Reyes had come aboard sometime earlier that night.

Launch time was nearing.

———

Orion's loading and storage bay was a flurry of movement. Loader bots filled with processed food and secondary equipment made their automated ways from storage bays to the ship, their movement a frictionless dance performed on superconducting pads that kept them hovering above the floor.

The ceiling was domed, easily twenty meters tall and lined with piping that carried the flow of fluids, ventilation, and information that Aldrin Station needed to operate. Voices jumbled into a low hum that echoed in the chamber.

Torrance liked coming here because it was a place he could see a hundred systems all working together. The bay was like a strange creation of quantum clockwork. Every piece was designed as an individual component, and yet, together they were the basic DNA of the ship. Take one part out, and something would break.

Today he was dead tired, and still the craft was magnificent.

A voice came from behind. "Have a good flight, Commander."

Torrance started, but recovered adequately to find Admiral Umaro standing in the corridor beside him.

"Thank you, Admiral."

"Are you all right?" she asked.

"Yes, I'm fine. Just didn't expect to see you down here."

"I like to see my crews off," she said as if to dismiss the topic. "I understand you've fixed H-MADS."

"'Fixed' may be a bit too generous, but, yes, it's working well enough to support the mission. Captain Douglas approved the approach fifteen minutes ago."

"Excellent. My trust in you has already paid off."

"Just doing my best, Admiral."

Umaro stared as a pallet loaded with refrigerated boxes whooshed past. Her hands were clasped behind her.

"I hope you'll take this the right way, Commander," she said in a low voice. "But doing your best isn't good enough now."

"I understand."

"Yes," she said. "I'm sure you do. At least I know I don't need to tell you how far Universe Three might be prepared to take this."

He flashed on the image of Marisa.

"No, Admiral, you don't."

"It is very important that we arrive at a reasonable peace before U3 gains the ability to destroy us. Otherwise we will find ourselves in the middle of the coldest of Cold Wars imaginable."

"Or the hottest of Hot Wars," Torrance added.

"Yes," she replied. "That would be the other option."

They stood for a moment, watching the bay work.

"I'll be off, Commander," the admiral said. "My skiff back to Kensington arrives in a few minutes."

"Thank you for stopping by, Admiral."

"You're welcome. Fly well."

Torrance gave the admiral a quick salute, which she returned prior to walking away.

CHAPTER 12

U3 Ship *Einstein*, Eta Cassiopeia System
Local Date: Conejo 4, 9
Local Time: 0630

t was early in the morning, but Casmir Francis had already been awake for hours. He had taken a skimmer to *Einstein* last night in preparation for the launch, and completed his full and unannounced inspection. He was pleased. The people understood how important this was, and they had been prepared.

Now he stood in the receiving bay control room, waiting for the nearby shuttle to arrive with the captives. He wanted to see them for himself. Wanted to know they were healthy and in good shape. They would be returned to the UG as a reward for playing nice—assuming UG played nice, anyway. He wanted to know his side of the bargain was being kept.

Casmir took an easy breath, which was amazing in itself. Atropos clearly agreed with him. The pressure of a C-Pak pulled across the skin of his left arm, and he remembered Yvonne's admonitions.

Waiting, he thought about the order of events for the meeting.

It was scripted to the minute.

In the old days, they would have used impulse power to get across the system, but seven years of experience had honed their jump algorithms to a more precise art.

Today, in less than an hour, *Einstein* and *Icarus* would jump to Galopar, and their net of skimmers would deploy. An hour later, UG's *Orion* would appear.

"Shuttle Pilot Gage requesting approval to dock," a voice called over the radio.

"I've got you on spotter, Gage," the reply came.

Einstein's doors opened to reveal dark space.

The shuttle edged into position, and the doors crawled closed. Air flooded the bay, and then four men and three women were escorted out of the tiny craft. All but one walked on their own—but the one, a man, tall and sun-marked, with unruly dark hair and a welt along the side of his head, was accompanied by an escort forcibly holding one arm.

"Who is he?" Casmir said to the bay steward.

She checked her register.

"I think that's one of the pilots," she replied.

Casmir squinted.

"Ah, yes. I remember him. Nimchura. We gave him his freedom years ago."

"Yes, sir," the steward said.

In the docking bay, the guards led the captives away, deeper into *Einstein*.

It was time, he thought, glancing at the clock on his sleeve's display. Actually, past time. He would have to move quickly if he was going to get to the bridge in time for the light show.

———

Nimchura was the last captive to step out of the shuttle and into *Einstein*'s cargo bay. Each of them had been assigned a personal guard. His guard's fingers were like a vise around his biceps, but unless someone was being particularly observant, to the outside world it would look like he was just helping Nimchura through the air lock. Nimchura admitted he was impressed by that. It took a certain degree of skill to control someone like this man was controlling him.

He also admitted that for a moment on the shuttle trip here his breath had been taken away when he first caught sight of *Einstein* through the shuttle's front screens. It had been a long time since he had seen an Excelsior class ship this close, and as God was his old-and-probably-dead Auntie's witness, the spacecraft's sleek configuration was a beautiful thing. The image hit Nimchura someplace deep in the gut—a place where emotions that ranged from envy to embarrassment to anger all gathered together in ways that made him numb.

Pretty much the entire shuttle got quiet for a moment when her gleaming white body first appeared.

But then they had landed and the ship's artificial gravity system had gathered them all up, and everyone, including Todias Nimchura, quickly got their wits back around them.

Which for Nimchura meant he was back to being pissed off.

"What are we doing here?" he said, breaking the silence he had been warned to hold.

"You'll be briefed when it's proper," his guard replied.

"I hear we're going home," Winni Paschel said as the shuttle touched down in *Einstein*'s bay.

"Shut up," her guard replied.

The sound of doors closing rumbled through the frame of the craft.

Winni had been a ranger who landed in the attack force. Unlike Nimchura, though, she had never played well with others, and hence had never been outside a cell for the full seven years they had been on Atropos. Her cheek carried a self-made tattoo in bleeding red ink, and her short hair had been recently "styled" to the best of someone's ability—mostly razored, with a tufted peak of red left to curl down over her forehead.

Whatever was happening, it was big.

Universe Three had cleaned them all up, and issued them each fresh duds. Clean pants and shirts. Polished shoes, and jackets that matched. It made him feel like they were all dressed up and ready for cotillion.

The shuttle door opened.

"On your feet."

That's when his guard put the clamps on his arm and led him forward. He was last in line, probably because they figured he had already been subdued once—or maybe because they didn't want his bruised cheekbone to be toward the front.

Winni's words bounced around in his head.

Could she be right? Were they going back to the UG?

He didn't understand much of what had happened to him in the past few hours, but it almost made sense that something like that could be happening. A prisoner transfer maybe—that was one of the scenarios the captives had all discussed back in the first days after the attack had failed. "How many U3 traitors are you worth?" was a game they played until (1) it got boring, and (2) it became obvious there wasn't going to be any miracle trade coming to save their asses.

But now they were all gathered together and being herded down the utility corridor of one of U3's Excelsior spacecraft.

He had been assigned on *Orion* for months back in the day.

He knew its layout like the back of his hand. They were walking down utility corridor C, a central path out of the main docking bay. Heading to pass several base systems and toward the temporary quarters. If they were being stored someplace, that made sense, he supposed.

As they walked through the ship, the idea of a trade now began to play on his mind.

The idea bothered him.

Why now?

Where the hell was this kind of thing earlier?

He thought about Hadri. Would she even want to come with him? What if she did? He didn't know how he felt about that. Until now he hadn't realized how much he had given up as he forced himself to become comfortable with a life spent pouring concrete. It was easy to get complacent when the world around you treated you with such indifference, but it annoyed him. All of it. He had decided that

Universe Three wasn't any better than the UG, but the same could be said the other way around. What if he was going back to them? What then? Another string of media events, UG military leaders sucking the soul from him for their PR benefit? Eating him up until there wasn't anything left? Nimchura thought about Deuce Jarboe. Really thought about him for the first time in a while. Remembered the shit-eating grin Deuce could get when he was screwing around with a journalist, and remembered the pepper-spray of debris that clattered against Nimchura's Firebrand as he flew through what remained of his wing leader and his spacecraft.

His skin crawled as the column of captives marched through the corridor.

The chill of *Einstein*'s controlled environment didn't help. The carpet-muffled footsteps that clamored off the corridor walls felt ominous.

Screw them all.

He may just be small fry. Just a guy. But who the hell was anyone to tell him how he should run his life? Who the hell were they to parade him around like some kind of a show dog?

The line spread out before him.

He watched a hallway branch off.

They moved into a utility corridor, a segment of the ship that broke off into a series of small nooks and crannies filled with utility accesses, and that included passages that led to several smaller command centers.

The shuttle bays were down the aisle and around to the left.

He was at the back of the line.

They came to an opening to the left. Without conscious thought, Nimchura dropped his shoulder, rammed into his guard's side, and brought his fist up to the soft part of the man's gut, right below his xiphoid process. The air rushed out of his lungs in a single soft *ompfh* as Nimchura wrapped his opposite arm around the guard and dragged him quickly down the hall.

The man gave a silent, gaping gasp.

Nimchura brought his knee up, and drove the man's head into it.

The guard went limp as a sack of concrete.

If Nimchura's grip hadn't been sure, and if he hadn't been conditioned from years of hard labor, perhaps he would have dropped the man. And if that had happened, perhaps the falling of the body would have alerted others to the action. But Nimchura's grip was sure. He eased the dead weight to the ground without sound, then scampered down a hallway, making a quick right and a left, then finding an alcove across from a systems panel.

The showers, he thought—they would be safe.

Unless U3 had reconfigured the plumbing, there was a systems team restroom down the next hallway.

He edged out and checked the hallway to his left. Movement down the way. Standard. Two crew members going about their job.

How long did he have?

Too late to worry about that.

He stepped around the corner to the right and ran directly into a young woman who had been coming out of the command station.

"Oops," she said, chuckling as she caught him to keep them both from falling. "Sorry about that. Are you okay?"

"Yes," he said, considering his next steps.

"Jump time coming," she said, quickly. "Everyone's in a rush."

Then she strode away, checking a portable datapad.

She thought Nimchura was part of the crew. Amazing. He gulped down his pounding heart and headed toward the facilities.

Then he stopped.

No.

There was a better place to go.

One of the skimmer launch bays was nearby. Just a zig and a zag away, then a short walk down another corridor. Depending on how U3 did things, there might be a guard there, or might not.

But Nimchura didn't care.

A moment later he was zigging and zagging.

A lone guard stood at the entry gate, which he took care of with a nonchalant approach, a quick joke, and a right cross that came from somewhere south of Mississippi. He pressed the guy's palm to the control pad, and listened to the security gate pop open.

Then he stepped into the tight corridor that held eight rounded bulkheads and eight air locks, each with a Z-pad skimmer behind it. He took the first one, and hit the manual override.

The gate released its lock and the round door swiveled open.

He stepped onto the entry platform, a flat bit of flooring that served as both the back end of the skimmer and a transition gate between the Z-pad's docking air lock and the mother ship.

"Roger that," a voice came from nearby.

The pilot was only an arm's length away, sitting at the controls of the Z-pad skimmer, reading off the mission profile and going through prelaunch checks.

What the hell? Nimchura thought.

He hadn't expected the skimmers to be prepping.

He toggled the lock closed, and the door swung.

The pilot had been so intent on his mission that he hadn't noticed the intrusion.

Nimchura reached into a storage bay and pulled down the emergency kit. It opened with a click that was strong enough the pilot finally turned his head.

"What are you doing?"

Nimchura grabbed a capsule of painkiller from the kit. He dropped the rest, then plunged the delivery end of the packet into the man's shoulder. The pilot was already buckled in, and had limited movement.

A moment later, he was slumped in the seat.

"What was that, Mouser?" a voice came over the intercom.

Nimchura pulled the man's helmet from his head, and spoke into the microphone—putting on his calm tone.

"Running one more preflight," he said. "Hold just a moment."

"Roger that."

The man would be out for a while.

Nimchura unbuckled him. It took all his effort to drag his ass out of the cockpit, but he managed. A quick negotiation with himself led to him opening the back gate one more time, and dumping the pilot. He would rather take the chance of being found prior to getting himself launched than deal with a U3 pilot who woke up with a hangover afterward.

The door finally shut, and Nimchura crawled into the pilot seat. He put the helmet on, and glancing down at the controllers, toggled a diagnostic and his radio system. "We're green on preflight," he said in monotone, scanning the rest of the flight plan.

The entirety of what he saw filtered over him.

"Jump code called in five seconds," the controller radioed. "Four…"

A whole string of skimmers were prepping to be launched.

Targeting schemes were preplanned.

"Three…"

Holy shit, he thought as he looked at his target.

"Two…"

Nimchura's gaze flashed across the control panel to see his assigned position. He recognized Galopar.

"One…"

Holy shit, he thought again. What had he just stepped into?

"And we are go for jump to superluminal."

Holy shit.

CHAPTER 13

UGIS *Orion*
Local Date: January 25, 2215
Local Time: 0730

Torrance stood on *Orion*'s bridge as the rest of the crew prepared for launch. It was an open, brightly lit space the size of a classroom. The forward section was a clear screen to open space. Projectors displayed status on the glass. Men and women in dress grays sat at consoles or stood at ease, their holographic controls giving them visual feedback as they spoke softly and pointed to data that poured from readouts.

A star chart in the middle of the control center gleamed with yellow and white markings, their current position a crimson triangle. Their eventual destination, Eta Cassiopeia B—or more precisely, the free space around Galopar—was a turquoise blaze toward the edge of the display's field of view.

Orion would jump to arrive on station in just a few minutes.

Torrance had not slept, but a shower and several successes had left him feeling like a changed man.

After the endless stream of funerals and state functions it was good to be back on an operational ship.

"This is your first super-L, isn't it, Commander?"

He turned to see Ambassador Reyes standing behind him.

Despite the silvered tip to his hair, Reyes appeared younger than he was. His skin was smooth except around the corners of his eyes, and those eyes were wide and of a light brown tone that bordered between hazel and almost green when the light hit them just right. His smile was smooth and practiced, the same expression he wore in all his PR appearances, a simple pulling back of the corners of his lips. He was dressed in a flowing black coat over a collarless blue shirt, the coat piped with a silver runner on the sleeves and along the buttons, of which he had engaged only two. His pants were classic black.

"Yes, sir," Torrance said. "First super-L."

"You're in for a treat, then."

"I'm Commander Torrance Black," he said too quickly. He extended his hand and shook the ambassador's when it, too, was extended.

"Alberto Reyes," the ambassador said. "I am thrilled to finally meet you in person."

Torrance cleared his throat in a nervous gesture. He knew about Reyes from news reports. The ambassador was a lawyer by degree, but had worked for several companies straight from school before going into a string of purely diplomatic positions, positions that included dealing with Universe Three in the early days of asteroid belt wildcatting. He had been assigned this role for his relationship with Casmir Francis himself.

"I understand the view is spectacular," Torrance said.

The ambassador nodded, his eyes getting a faraway expression. "It is beyond my ability to describe. Perhaps we should enjoy it together."

"Sounds like a good idea. I can't wait to see it."

Torrance sat in one of the six observation chairs at the back of the bridge. The ambassador sat beside him.

"Launch positions in five minutes." Abke's voice came over the room.

Torrance was surprised to find his palms sweating.

They watched the crew work for another minute.

"Tell me," Torrance finally said. "How do you expect the negotiations to go?"

The ambassador shrugged. "I never predict."

"There are people around here who aren't entirely on your side, you know?"

"What side is that?"

"Well," Torrance said, trying to come up with something that sounded proper. "A lot of the crew have lost friends to U3. Some of those are hoping your negotiations prove fruitless."

"I suppose you're right."

Torrance pressed his lips together.

"What about you, Commander?" Reyes said. "You're *Everguard*'s hero. What do you think of my mission?"

"I don't know."

"That may be the most honest response I've ever heard."

Torrance shrugged off the compliment. "I see both positions, I guess. But I don't know. Intergalactic wars would seem to be hard to win."

"That's right. But they are also very hard to lose."

"What do you mean?"

Reyes was silent for a moment, as if considering things.

"Think about it, Torrance. You don't understand just how huge the galaxy is until you're out there."

"You're right about that," he said, looking out the observation screen into the darkness of space. "There are a lot of places to hide."

"And that is the problem," Reyes responded. "Especially when your opponent is small and mobile while your own population is very large, very easy to find, and quite limited in its ability to get around."

Torrance nodded, thinking about history and about entire cities that had been wiped out in single blasts. If U3 actually won a full-fledged war, the Solar System's primary civilizations would be sitting ducks.

"I hadn't thought of it that way. I suppose infinite hiding places give a group that doesn't want to get caught a lot of leeway. And I suppose hidden enemies can do a lot of damage."

The ambassador gave him an appraising glance that made Torrance uncomfortable.

"You are an interesting man, Commander Black. Are you sure you have found your true calling?"

"What do you mean?"

"Very few people can see things from more than one point of view, and those few are very important."

"How do you mean—"

"One minute to launch," Abke said over the comm system.

The crew came to a stand-down at their desks.

Their work was done, their "go" signals set. All that was left was to let it all happen.

Reyes settled back in his chair.

"Launch engines full thrust," Abke reported. "Multi-d gate toggle is on the timer. Five seconds. Four. Trim engines active. Two. One. Launch initiated."

"We are go for jump, Captain," the navigation desk said.

Torrance became amazed.

Colors bloomed red and green like Christmas lights and flowed in rivulets. A blue wave twisted into a ghostlike dragon before disappearing. Green lighting clapped to the oohs and aahs of the crew. Energy billowed like time-lapse photos of thunder clouds. Stars became yellow flares.

Torrance sat in slack-jawed wonder. "How long does it last?" he finally managed.

"Until we drop out of FTL," Reyes replied.

"My God."

"Yes. I'm sure it's something like that."

Neither spoke from that point on.

THE MESSAGE

CHAPTER 14

U3 Ship *Einstein*, Z-pad Launch Bay, Galopar orbit
Local Date: Conejo 4, 9
Local Time: 0645

Nimchura wrapped his hand over the Z-pad's joystick, trying to remember the craft's technical specs as the seconds ticked past. He had flown a Z-pad before, but it had been more than a while. He remembered the crafts' higher-order specs. Powered by a pair of CuttCo engines. Built more for escort than attack, and as such was focused on maneuverability rather than speed. It meant he probably couldn't outrun a real fighter, but he could essentially stop on a dime.

Along those lines, he let his eyes scan the control panels above him where a row of toggles that engaged trim boosters had been built into the framework of the fuselage.

The central plasma cannon was armed and fully charged. He had two laser weapons mounted on each side of his cockpit pod, which was round and transparent, which, assuming he dropped radiation shields, would give him a view of space that would make him feel like he was sitting on a flat platter—though why he would drop his radiation shields was beyond him. He may be an idiot flyboy, but he really wasn't carrying a death wish.

The mission timer counted down.

"We are out of super-L," the controller called. "Thirty seconds to launch."

"Roger," came the voice of a pilot.

"Roger," came another, then another, and another, until there was a pregnant pause.

"Mouser?"

"Roger," Nimchura said, filling the space.

"Roger," came another voice.

He squeezed the joystick.

The good news was that the base launch sequence and mission setup was preprogrammed—whoever had developed the profile was thorough and focused on details. The eight Z-pads here would be spaced out along a single line.

The bad news was that the target was clearly *Orion*.

"Five seconds."

What was going on? Was he going to destroy *Orion*?

The launch system engaged.

Ahead of him, the pod bay doors irised open. A moment later g forces pressed him into his seat and he was flying again, racing through deep space on the back of a piece of machinery built to burn plasma.

For just that one moment, those questions didn't matter.

Per the mission plan, the Z-pad's autopilot took hold of his skimmer at first, maneuvering him to his assigned station in space. So he spent time listening to the familiar sound of radio chatter. The skimmer pilots were raw, untested, and nervous. He could hear that in their voices.

He took a few minutes to get more reacquainted with the instrument panel. It splayed in from of him in dim red and green hues—thruster controls, direct interfaces to the computer system that plugged into his helmet and monitored his physical parameters to adjust everything from the compartment's temperature to the softness of the seating. A navigation pane scrolled up on the screen, and he saw the locations of each skimmer as well as *Einstein*.

A battle map showed him *Icarus*, posted at a position opposite Galopar, which showed as a huge green and orange ball that loomed in space before him.

Memories of his months planetside came back.

He remembered how it felt to be working so hard and not be able to fly, and it immediately compared to his time on Atropos. The difference was that on Galopar he knew he was working toward a mission, whereas gaining his "freedom" on Atropos meant slinging concrete for the rest of his life.

"Target due on station in fifteen seconds," a voice came from the radio.

"Roger, command lead," came the lone reply.

The timer marked the passage of each second.

For a moment, Nimchura forgot to breathe.

Then a shimmer came to space in front of him. A pinprick of a warp at first, then a wavering form that bent the star pattern around him. There was no sound, of course. No boom. Just a dim flare of light, and the sudden appearance of the spacecraft.

Orion had arrived.

CHAPTER 15

UGIS *Orion*
Local Date: January 25, 2215
Local Time: 0815

mmediately upon dropping out of superluminal, Captain Douglas met with his staff. The briefing room held twelve people in relative comfort. Torrance was the fifteenth to enter.

Feeling out of place, he picked his way to stand against the corner along the left side of the oblong table. Two officers were already standing; the rest were seated and chatting quietly.

Ambassador Reyes sat to the left of the captain's empty chair.

Two officers broke out in laughter over a joke Torrance hadn't heard.

Captain Douglas entered and all discussion stopped.

"Universe Three is here," he said, stepping straight to his place and getting directly to the point. "*Einstein* is on our short-range radio sensors. They have also positioned a network of skimmers across space. I think it's safe to assume their weapons are trained on us—though I think it's unlikely they can cause us serious damage."

Torrance knew better than ask what Douglas meant by "serious damage," but he also understood weapons systems well enough now to know that a Z-pad's plasma cannons could create a serious crimp in *Orion*'s style.

"We do not know the location of *Icarus*," the captain continued.

He punched a touchpad on the desk. The holo created an image of Atropos. A blazing red blip represented *Orion* and a blue mark represented *Einstein*, who sat on a bearing directly between *Orion* and U3's home planet. "Per the agenda, we will be receiving guests in less than an hour, so the ambassador has something he wants to say."

Douglas motioned to Reyes. "Ambassador Reyes?"

The ambassador rose.

"I know how hard this is for many of you," Reyes said. "But our mission is clear. As representatives of our government, I expect we will treat our visitors with dignity and grace."

Torrance saw suppressed anger.

After what seemed like a week of silence, the commander from secondary propulsion spoke what everyone else had been thinking. "I can't believe we're going to have Casmir Francis aboard our ship, and we're not going to do a goddamned thing about it."

"This is a mission of peace," the ambassador said.

"What if *they* ambush *us*?" another commander asked.

Captain Douglas leaned in before the ambassador could respond. "Thanks to our resident war hero, we have our H-MADS system operational. And standard battle orders will be observed throughout the negotiation." Douglas paused just long enough to ensure everyone was listening. "Please review them, now."

Arms reached out in unison, fingers pressing display pads to bring up the appropriate battle specs. Torrance scanned his quickly: Armed crew members were to be at every power station and environmental control command; sensor scans were to be at 100 percent pattern matching. All weaponry was armed and ready.

Douglas gave them time to read before continuing.

"We'll be at the rendezvous point in a half hour. Which means we need everybody prepared and at their stations in fifteen minutes. But I want to reiterate what the ambassador said. This is a peaceful mission. A lot of lives depend on how we perform today. Let's not blow it."

———

Z-pad
    Local Date: Conejo 4, 9
    Local Time: 0700

Nimchura watched the shuttle disembark from *Einstein*.

What in the hell was happening?

"Thunderbolt has left the Professor," came the radio call. "All weapons on lockdown."

Nimchura's fingers played across the panel as he set his plasma cannon to focus on *Orion*'s Star Drive system. That was the plan, and he didn't want to draw attention by deviating now.

What was happening, though?

Why were they locking on a spaceship that one of their shuttles was so obviously getting ready to board? Was this some kind of mutiny? Was the U3 space force working with the UG now? What was in the shuttle? People? Material? Information? He interpreted the Professor as the radio call sign of *Einstein*, but what, or who, was Thunderbolt?

All he knew for sure was that Universe Three had a string of skimmers lined up on two sides, ready to attack.

And all he could think about now was that several hundred crew on *Orion* were sitting ducks in these crosshairs. Just like the crews on *Sunchaser* and *Everguard* had been.

He let his gaze play out over space, saw the line of bright dots that represented the Z-pads, each sitting on that line like a buzzard with a plasma cannon.

His throat grew big, and he swallowed down a dry mouth.

His fingers played along the control panel almost as if they were working on their own, calling up the weapons controllers, and adjusting the laser systems and his central targeting system.

Then he pulled up navigation.

As the shuttle from *Einstein* entered *Orion*'s docking bay, Nimchura's work came to a close.

He may not know what was happening, but he knew what he was going to do.

Remember the goddamned *Sunchaser*, assholes.

Remember Deuce Jarboe.

———

Torrance sat in his command office and watched *Einstein*'s shuttle arrive on intership video. A detachment of Universe Three security exited the shuttle first, then what he assumed were officers of the organization, and then Casmir Francis himself exited.

The man's appearance twisted in his gut.

Torrance was running on pure adrenaline by now, but felt emotionally dizzy. His brain was fogged by lack of sleep, but his entire body was amped up and reacting to the smallest of inputs.

It would be so easy to take this man out here.

Casmir Francis—the man who was single-handedly responsible for the deaths of people Torrance had served with for the past fifteen local years.

He thought about Malloy and Marisa.

He thought about Alexandir Romanov and his son Andre. The captain had planned to retire after he conned *Everguard* to its final resting bay. His son would have followed through with his career.

The desire for vengeance was suddenly strong.

On the other hand, the ambassador's words about the position that the United Government found themselves in came back to Torrance, too. They were true enough—with the spread of humanity across the stars, there really was no way to truly win an intergalactic war, but there were thousands of ways to lose one.

In the quiet of the moment, he flashed on the idea of life on Eden, whatever it might be.

He had been so busy since the *Everguard* disaster, that other than that one afternoon, the Eden files hadn't really entered his consciousness. But now he was filled with sensations that were equal parts hope and dread. If human beings couldn't come to a peace with other human beings, what chance did they have to come to understandings with truly alien cultures?

Suddenly he found himself hoping beyond hope that Reyes managed to pull this off.

Einstein's shuttle cleared the loading bay door.

Torrance pulled his glance from the systems controls to focus on the real-time video feed. A few moments from now, Casmir Francis and his party would walk out of the landing bay and down the corridor to the meeting hall, where he would meet Ambassador Reyes. They would shake hands and begin working on what was arguably the most important treaty in the history of the galaxy.

Everything snapped into focus.

His heart thundered in his chest.

He was confused at first, then angry, then quite terrified.

He replayed the glances he had seen pass between officers in the briefing room, remembered the harshness of Douglas's words as he moved up milestones in the mission. He thought about the error they had been working on—the motion that caused the faulty trigger was exactly that of a man accepting a handshake.

Something snapped inside his brain.

Holy Christ.

This was all a big ruse.

The trigger had never been faulty. He hadn't had time to actually review the root code, but he was willing to bet anything at all that the system was working exactly as it had been programmed to work.

Torrance glanced at the clock as he ran from his office and raced through the corridor. He didn't know if he could make it in time, but he had to get to Weapons Command.

If he didn't stop them, life as they knew it might well be over.

CHAPTER 16

Z-pad, Galopar orbit
Local Date: Conejo 4, 9
Local Time: 0715

Nimchura finished reprogramming the weapons controller, and then deactivated the mission profile.

"What are you doing, Mouser?"

He ignored the question, and engaged the CuttCo drives. The trim boosters flared, sending a thrumming through the compartment as the rockets rotated him into a direction along the line of Z-pads before him. *Einstein* lay at the end of that line.

He hoped he made it that far.

Twisting the joystick, he drove the Z-pad hard forward. False gravity pressed him against his seat, making him smile. If he was going to die, at least it was going to be on his own terms.

"Mouser, please report."

The first Z-pad came to bear. He took it with a laser blast to its fuel cell. A steady roll got him past the debris field. He pulled his skimmer up, and targeted Z-pad number two.

Chatter filled his ears as it exploded.

He got the third before the rest began to react.

Nimchura's assessment of the pilots had been right. They were green, and they were nervous—more concerned with managing their mission profiles than able to fly their spacecraft. He picked two more off before the collective got themselves together. By this time the radio frequency had changed, and the chatter went dead.

"Disconnect all auto input," Nimchura commanded—just in case central command had any remote tricks up their sleeves.

Five of *Einstein*'s Z-pads remained.

His sensor system reported that a group of *Icarus*'s craft were being deployed into his sector.

He let his mind flow into the craft.

Let his body become the deflector plates and flow into the heat of the engines. The hydraulics became blood that ran in his veins. The smell of the craft was something solid then, permeated his being, became part of the thing that he was, merged with the brine of his sweat and the earthy tone of the Universe Three jacket he was wearing.

He put the craft into a sharp eight-point roll at the same time as he twisted across *Einstein*'s plane of fire. The craft responded beautifully. He dropped speed, then bumped it up, targeting another Z-pad, and seeing it disintegrate before him. This was what he was meant to do, he thought, almost in passing. This was who he was, he knew as he pulled on the joystick and screamed against g forces that would kill a person of lesser conditioning.

His systems flashed red as tails locked onto him.

He waggled and swooped, losing the lock, but also losing a target.

A Z-pad became framed in the green of the planet, and he blazed it.

Icarus's Z-pads arrived.

Nimchura took out three of them, but there were too many.

He understood he was doomed as four of them blocked his backside, and two more flew ropes around his flanks.

He understood he wasn't going to get a clean shot at *Einstein* as he dove for the protective floor of Galopar's atmospheric shell.

That didn't matter anymore, though.

He was flying.

He was driving a machine through space as hard as he could drive it. Sitting on the edge of his capability.

Doing what he was made to do.

He was flying this piece-of-shit skimmer in ways it had never been flown before.

For a moment, he thought he was going to make it.

The sensors showed he hit the upper ionosphere of Galopar's shell. Another moment and he would begin entry. Another moment and he was certain that the green pilots of the Universe Three space force would never be able to follow him.

The shot that took out his portside deflector shields changed all that.

A moment later Todias "Yuletide" Nimchura lost control of his skimmer, and plunged into the upper layers of Galopar's atmosphere.

CHAPTER 17

UGIS *Orion*
Local Date: January 25, 2215
Local Time: 0910

"Skiles?" Torrance said into his personal communicator while he shouldered his way through the routine foot traffic in the main corridor. With every step he was moving faster, but his heart was pounding at three times the speed of his feet.

"Sir?"

"I need the parameter that H-MADS's image processing system uses to trigger data to the laser."

"What are you doing, sir?"

"Just get me the goddamned parameter," he cried, growing short of breath.

His chest hurt as he ran. His legs burned.

He bounced off people as he turned corners and jumped into the central lift tube where he bent over with his hands on his knees, panting while it slowly moved him deeper into *Orion*'s belly. Ten seconds had never felt so long.

"I've sent the parameter to your memory space, sir," Skiles replied.

"Thank you, Lieutenant." Torrance checked the system on his handheld. Yes, the code was there, a long binary string with a randomly named alphanumeric key that was running right alongside the normal security watchdog. Yuan was very, very good.

"May I ask again what you're doing, sir?" Skiles asked.

"Nothing," he said. He didn't know who was in on this. Maybe everyone? Or just a small conspiracy? Just Yuan? Suddenly the world seemed to crash in on him. He couldn't afford to tell Skiles anything. That was the problem with conspiracies, he realized. Once you knew something was going on, you couldn't be sure of anything.

The lift door opened. He ran.

Weapons Command was just down the hallway.

He burst in, the door crashing against the back wall with a lightning bolt's clap.

Faces turned to him, slack with surprise.

His breathing was ragged, and his hair disheveled. A bead of sweat rolled down his temple.

LiJuan Yuan was there, her hair prim and proper, her makeup precise. She had been watching a screen that displayed an image of Casmir Francis emerging from the pod, surrounded by an entourage of guards in brown and white.

"I want you to show me the H-MADS triggering routines," he said to the ensign working the prime weapons console.

The ensign made no direct move.

"I said show me the triggering code."

"Universe Three is aboard this ship, Commander," Yuan said. "We don't have time for that."

"I'm sure you don't," Torrance said with too much force. He stomped to the prime console. "But as your commanding officer I direct you to show me the triggering routines."

"It's too late, Commander. There's nothing you can do."

Torrance's gaze whipped back to Yuan.

"H-MADS wasn't failing at all, was it?"

"No," she said. "Quite the opposite."

"You configured a second code path that hijacked the trigger command. The standard path looked intact, but never actually got executed, but your hijack code triggered just fine."

"You really are very bright, Commander."

"All of our problems these past few days were because H-MADS was intentionally triggering the hallway weapons system."

"Worked like a charm, didn't it?" Yuan said with a gleeful smile. "You should have listened when I said there was nothing wrong with Weapons Systems."

Torrance saw a certain measure of elegance in what they had done.

When Casmir Francis met Ambassador Reyes, he would move to shake hands, which would be passed through the image processor. The H-MADS would catch it, of course. And that would trigger…yes, elegance. Sadistic elegance. Casmir Francis himself would act as the trigger for his own world's demise.

"What are you targeting now?" he asked with a deadpan voice.

"Atropos City." The masculine voice came from behind him. "Their manufacturing plant, to be exact."

Torrance blanched.

"Captain Douglas," he said, turning.

"At your service."

"That city has thousands of people living there."

"Maybe you and your ambassador can live with what happened to *Everguard*, Commander Black. But some of us have other ideas in mind."

"Who else is in this?"

"I hope you'll understand why I'll refrain from answering that question. And also what we mean when I say that we're all hoping the infamous Torrance Black can be counted on to be one of us."

"I don't understand. Why go through all this when you could just fire?"

Yuan and Douglas shared a glance. Yuan spoke.

"H-MADS has had a string of well-documented failures, Commander. And after today, it will be obvious that this was just another—very unfortunate—systems error that triggered the main plasma weapon, which, as a standard precaution had, of course, been targeted at Atropos City. It will be an accident of terrible proportions, but a useful one."

Douglas walked casually to the center of the room.

"Commander Black, do you remember when we first met and Admiral Umaro said that her advisers didn't think you can win a galactic war?"

"Of course."

"We're going to prove them wrong. We're putting an end to this forever."

"Which was impossible without being able to get into point-blank range and with *Icarus* or *Einstein* always on full alert," Yuan finished.

Douglas gave her a sharp glance.

"I admit that Umaro's little diplomatic mission was helpful in that fashion. This gives us one clean shot."

Torrance shook his head. Thousands of people would die.

What could he do, though?

The primary weapons console loomed beside him. It felt cold, and distant. Weapons Command's primary targeting parameters were all controlled through that interface, which was accessed through panels in the upper ring of the room. If he could get there, he could change them—to what, he didn't know—maybe he could have the shot dissipate into open space.

Captain Douglas drew up before him.

"All you have to do, Commander Black, is keep your mouth shut like a good little war hero, and you'll be set for life."

"I understand," he said.

The captain moved to pat him on the shoulder. "I knew you wouldn't let us down."

Before he knew what he was doing, Torrance let fly a right cross that caught Douglas under the chin. He spun and crashed into an ensign, then raced up the stairs to the console. The controller was ready for him, but Torrance grabbed him and, in a fit of strength he didn't know he had, threw the man across the room and into a guard who had been drawing his hand weapon. Screaming voices echoed in the compartment, but Torrance couldn't make them out.

He turned to the console and logged in through the retinal scanner. The targeting data glared in crimson numbers.

Yuan's screaming voice came from the haze.

She crashed into him, raking at his face, but she was too slim to knock him away and he gave a quick turn to throw her aside.

He changed numbers at random, then closed the entry screen. "Access priority on my voice cross-referenced to that of Marisa Harthing," he said into the system, adding the first name that came to his mind.

"Access control modified to the voice of Black, Torrance, Commander, Interstellar Command, and Harthing, Marisa, Lieutenant, Interstellar Command."

The room grew deathly quiet.

He had managed it. Had changed the targeting parameters, and hopefully saved Atropos City. No one could get in to change them, not without both Torrance's and Marisa's voice patterns. Now he just had to figure out what came next.

"God damn you," the captain said, now standing up and rubbing his jaw. "I'll have you court-martialed for this."

Torrance laughed. "And the charge will be…refusing to accept a direct command of a mutinous officer? I can hear the Ag Gen now, Captain. '*And what order did he fail to follow?*'"

His cheek burned where Yuan had scratched him.

He reached up and found he was bleeding.

"No, Captain," Torrance said. "I think it'll be best for everyone involved to just leave here as if nothing happened."

"Sir?" an ensign said. He was staring at the console as if it had begun leaking radioactive material. "Uh, I don't think that's going work, either."

"Yes?"

"Those coordinates. Unless I miss my mark, they are along a line of sight to *Einstein*."

"Shit," Douglas said.

"Maybe it will miss," Torrance said.

"No," Yuan replied with an expression that was almost a smile. "You're not a real weapons officer, so you wouldn't think about the target refinement algorithms we have built into the system. It will adjust to whatever it finds."

Torrance ignored the insult. He had read about the algorithms Yuan was talking about—interfaces to the sensors systems that took direct targeted vectors and compared them to real-time threat movements. The coordinates he had coded would be massaged by this system, and it would adjust them to refine the targets to any hostile craft it found.

"The shot will destroy *Einstein*," Torrance finally said.

"We've got to get the hell out of here before the system triggers," the captain said.

Torrance understood the panicked expression on Douglas's face. The first Eta Cass incident taught them a lot about what happened when a Star Drive system was destroyed. It would implode through the dimensions, and there was a reasonable chance that the blowback could damage the Star Drive gates if their feeds were nearby.

Torrance looked at Yuan. Yuan looked at the captain.

They all moved at once.

"Abke," the captain said, already heading for the doorway. "Patch this through to the bridge. All hands prepare for immediate jump to super-L. Destination Miranda Station. Call the jump as soon as ready. Do not wait for my command, repeat, do not wait for my command."

UGIS *Orion* Assembly Room
 Local Date: January 25, 2215
 Local Time: 0915

At the same time the captain was relaying that order, Casmir Francis, who had boarded *Orion* ten minutes prior, approached Ambassador Reyes.

The ambassador's conference center was long and narrow with a high ceiling. Blue and red flags of both the United Government and Universe Three draped the walls.

Hushed voices whispered in low tones.

Casmir felt the air against his skin, the breath entering his nostrils, his chest expanding. The fabric of his clothes rasped as they brushed together with each of his strides, and the creaking and jingling of his guards' boots and weapons came in the same rhythm.

The ambassador stood on a raised stage at the far end of the room, flanked by two aides. His expression was professionally neutral, but even that gave Casmir comfort.

Today they would make history for all of humankind.

The years of fighting had made Casmir old and tired, but they had been worth it, because this moment was everything he had ever dreamed of. His people were going to be freed forever.

He climbed the lowest stairs and came to the stage. As he moved to cross from the left, Ambassador Reyes of the UG walked in from the right. They met at the center.

The ambassador extended his hand in welcome, and Casmir raised his as well.

———

Monitors recorded Casmir Francis's movement.

Software systems transformed it into binary codes, toggled switches, and system commands. The three main energy weapons mounted at triangular distance around *Orion*'s shell swiveled to draw their beads on *Einstein*.

Then they fired.

Streams of plasma and antiplasma flared.

A moment later, *Orion* went superluminal.

CHAPTER 18

UGIS *Orion*
Local Date: January 25, 2215
Local Time: 0920

The ambassador's hand was warm in Casmir's grasp. The smile on the man's face was now a bit forced, which was to be expected from a diplomat. He didn't think there was an ambassador in existence who ever had a genuine emotion.

Casmir turned to face the gathering of UG security forces that appeared beside Reyes.

U3 guards shouldered their weapons with a cascade of metallic clatter.

"What is this?" Casmir Francis said.

Ambassador Reyes frowned and looked genuinely perplexed.

"Come with us, Director Francis," the UG security leader said.

The crowd murmured and began to scramble about.

"Stop this," Reyes yelled above the din.

The first shot from the U3 laser missed Casmir. That goodness for nerves. He ducked to avoid any others, and ran for the doorway, his guards hunched over and spewing laser fire as they followed. The corridor outside was filled with white-clad United Government soldiers.

Son of a…

He glanced over his shoulder and saw his U3 soldiers in the meeting hall were trapped. A crimson laser took one of his guards in the chest, and the young man crumpled with an anguished cry. More voices clamored in a rising wave of sound. His security officers pushed him down the hallway, and Casmir almost fell.

A flash of memory came: Perigee's Lunar pyramid from so long ago. Bodies falling. Voices calling out in fear over the squawk of the radio.

He would be trampled, he thought as he pushed himself from a wall.

This can't be happening.

He was too close to his dream to lose it now.

Too close.

He shook himself free of the security detail and stepped forward, hands raised.

"Stop this!"

The shot came from the left of the auditorium. It caught him just over the hip. The burning sensation was like a billion ants biting, crawling, and swarming up over his side and then his chest. His teeth ground together. A molar broke with biting pain. He may have screamed or he may not have. All he knew was that he was writhing on the floor and wishing for all his life that he would die and be put out of this misery.

Another shot hit his shoulder.

A final blast granted his wish.

FALLOUT

SOURCE: INFOWAVE — NEWS for the twenty-third century
DATE: January 25, 2215, Earth Standard
HEADLINE: Casmir Francis, Terrorist Leader, Dies in Hospital

Casmir Francis was pronounced dead at 0955 this morning at Aldrin Station Medical Center after valiant attempts to save his life failed. Francis had been wounded during the ill-fated peace conference that UG officials had requested, which was being held aboard the Orion.

"Mr. Francis died of extensive tissue damage as a result of plasma fire," said Dr. Melinda Dermott, chief of emergency medicine. "Every effort was made to resuscitate him, and he fought hard to live. But the damage was too great."

The mood at the station was somber, but protests have broken out in the streets of several cities and on several college campuses where Francis is often portrayed as an icon for those concerned with civil liberty.

The president is scheduled to make comments tomorrow morning. There is no word yet whether services will be held, nor has the Universe Three command responded to news of Francis's death.

"We intend to transport the director's body back to the Eta Cassiopeia system if Universe Three forces will let us," said General Ophelia Nichols.

CHAPTER 19

Atropos, Eta Cassiopeia System
Local Date: Conejo 4, 9
Local Time: 0725

Deidra Francis pressed her hands against the second-floor command room's windowsill and stared out at Eta Cass to the east. The sleeves of her white shirt were rolled up, and the last rays of the day fell on her freckled forearms. She was here because her father wanted a leader on the ground, but she didn't like this.

The UG offer was bad karma, but her father was stubborn just like she was, and his council was so weak in the spine that it was a goddamned joke.

Perhaps her parents had been radicals in the days of their youth, but now, after being on their own for so long, they had grown old and soft in the middle. And their advisers were worse. In the end they agreed with Papa on this issue just as they did on any decision these days. It all added up to say that Universe Three had traded one government for another that was equally weak.

That was what Deidra was thinking as she let her gaze climb to the point in the sky where *Einstein* would be meeting *Orion*. The sky was clear enough now that if it were nighttime the ships would be a pair of glimmering white dots with probably a quarter degree separation between them and the planet.

It was not yet dark, though, so the sky was merely a cloudy blue.

A pair of blue-winged birds native to Atropos raced in a current.

Her stomach ached with tension.

The scuffing of footsteps and the nearly silent hum of computer machinery came from the room behind her. A few voices merged into the background of her fatigue.

"Are you okay?" Matt Anderson said from a few steps behind her.

"I'm fine."

"I could get you a drink or something."

"I said I'm fine."

Anderson was always around her these days, and it didn't take a genius to know that his primary interest was getting into her pants—just the idea made her angry. Hell, he was nearly thirty.

He stepped closer to her. He smelled like soap.

"Your father's going to be all right."

"I don't trust them."

"You should get something to eat," Matt said.

"I'm not hungry."

"You haven't eaten all day."

"That's all right, I'm making up for it by not sleeping tonight."

Matt laughed too loud.

She looked at the sky again, then the clock. The real discussions wouldn't start for another hour.

A light flared high in the sky. At first Deidra thought she was seeing things, but it bloomed across the horizon brightly and quickly. Her heart dropped, and she gripped the sill until her fingers turned white.

"Holy shit," a male voice bellowed.

"What is it?" she said, turning away from the window and shouldering her way past Anderson. The communications post didn't respond. "Tell me," she said. "What's happening?" Blue and green light flashed from the holo display. "Tell me, goddamn it."

The display ran with numbers and flashed with red warning posts about loss of signal from every system on board *Einstein*.

When the comm controller turned to look at her, his face was ashen, his jaw slack.

"Son of a bitch!" she said, looking at noise that covered the comm screen. "I knew we couldn't trust them! Son of a bitch! Son of a goddamned bitch!"

CHAPTER 20

Galopar
Local Date: Undefined
Local Time: Undefined

Nimchura's Z-pad fell through layers of atmosphere in what would be called *reentry* under most other circumstances, but what he called full-tilt, balls-out, crash mode. A wall of plasma fire flowed over the cockpit shield. The sound of scrubbing air grew thick in the tiny compartment as he bounced left and right, then pitched forward. He grabbed the joystick hard. Heat raised the temperature as Nimchura tried to correct his position, tried to get the craft to align properly, and at least make max use of his heat shields.

The Z-pad rotated, and a hard bottom nearly drove his stomach out his ass.

Thump.

The craft's starboard deflector shields grabbed air and spun him around.

Nimchura forced the joystick down, nearly passing out as the craft snapped to a forward attitude. He pitched himself even more forward.

The skimmer came out of a cloud, and he saw land and water.

The forward trim pods worked, and one of his engines still had fire.

No reason to wait.

He hit the trim pods to slow himself down. They boomed in the planet's thick air and sent plumes of smoke around him, but he had the ability to hold his craft almost steady—at least the corkscrew pattern he was falling with was partially adjustable.

He had a base plate of the deflectors on the portside, which he could use as a wing if he got the right pitch and yaw. The starboard engine was out, but portside actually had partial power, though it sputtered in and out. He turned the deflectors on the right wing set, and toggled the portside engine. The corkscrew slowed, and while he was still essentially falling, he found he could guide the direction of the fall, and even adjust his trajectory.

He was flying.

Guiding his craft, banking hard, using what resources he had to fly this piece of smoldering metal down through the atmosphere.

The joystick felt like it was connected directly to his brain as he aimed the skimmer toward the shoreline that sprawled out before him.

Nimchura smiled at that.

He has seen this shoreline before—on their test flights.

Though the craft would never make it that far, the old base was only a short hop away.

He took a deep breath, and tasted the coppery flavor of hope.

CHAPTER 21

Calisto Station Military Courthouse
Local Date: January 27, 2215
Local Time: 1630

nterstellar Command commenced an immediate inquiry into exactly what had happened and who was at fault.

Torrance sat in the back of the courtroom among several of *Orion*'s crew. Full attendance made the chamber feel small. The air seemed to be heavy and thick. The sound of the whole room felt muted.

Captain Douglas sat in an isolation box.

Commander Yuan and four other officers sat behind the captain.

The review panel arrived from a chamber behind the tribunal panel, each dressed in understated brown formals with their blue and silver medals flashing from flat shoulder pads.

Counsel for each defendant made perfunctory openings, and arguments began.

Torrance testified third, the ambassador fourth.

Military justice is not like civilian justice.

Yes, there are protocols. And, yes, there are enough arcane legal maneuvers and procedural details to be addressed that Torrance had a hard time keeping up and by the end of the day was tired and confused from making the effort.

But military justice does not stand on appeal. The answer is the answer. And in this case, the answer was succinct.

Captain Wallace Douglas was found guilty of mutiny, stripped of rank, dishonorably discharged, and sentenced to twenty years in the Lunar military correctional facility. Commander Yuan was also stripped of rank and dishonorably discharged. She would serve ten years. The others were stripped of rank and assessed charges against their performance records. For all essential purposes, their careers were finished.

It wasn't enough, of course. Not by a far sight.

Only thirty years between the whole set of collaborators, some probably to be commuted at some later date by a faceless military leader under the cloak of time.

The whole thing was sickening, really.

Torrance wondered what deals Yuan and Douglas had tried to make, and what deals two of the other officers had been successful at making that kept them out of jail.

Not that it mattered.

Torrance had seen the game played twice now, how at these times the ends justify the means and facts didn't matter as much as allegiances.

CHAPTER 22

Atropos, Eta Cassiopeia System
Local Date: Conejo 7, 9
Local Time: 1410

Deidra Francis stood in front of the empty chair at the head of the table. Even now, days after the disaster, she was unable to look at her father's advisers without feeling rage.

She should have been stronger. She should have stood her ground. If she had made them listen, perhaps her father would still be alive. Instead she had gotten caught up in their assurances, gotten her head full of the idea that she was being promoted when really she was just being put aside in a way that served to keep her quiet.

But she had been right, goddamn it.

Everyone else had been wrong.

"They want to return your father's body," Gregor Anderson said. The rest of the command staff sat in the dark room.

"No negotiations," she said to the gathering.

"The people will want him back."

"Tell that to the mothers and fathers and children of those we lost on *Einstein*."

"They say the destruction of *Einstein* was an accident," Martin Scalese said.

"And they are *so* trustworthy."

"The UG is offering—"

"I can't believe you, Martin. There wasn't a single survivor from *Einstein*. Not a single one. *Orion* left the area less than a quarter second before the blast would have ripped it to shreds. The perfection of this timing alone says that the operation had to be planned to a razor's edge—add to it that the precision of the blast that hit *Einstein* could not have been a mistake. Now they offer their apologies, and you actually think it's a good idea to listen to them?

"No.

"I don't trust the UG. Not in any fashion. Nothing they say is true.

"This is how we will think now."

The panel sat forward.

Deidra ran her hand through her hair as she gathered back her composure.

She glanced at her mother, who nodded with a thin-lipped expression of determination. Both had worked tirelessly trying to keep abreast of the situation, sleeping only in half-hour catnaps here and there, and always pushing the right buttons.

She looked at Gregor Anderson, who was sitting in his usual chair, but whose body seemed to be a shriveled shell now, covered by that wild beard of white that at one time had made him look wise, but now had faded to make him appear merely old.

"Your father would have—" Gregor said.

"My father is dead, and *Einstein* is gone. Both of these things are true because this panel didn't have the spine to advise him appropriately."

"How can you say that?"

"Because it's also true." She hesitated, staring across the set of eyes that filled the room. "You all know it, too. You're just not saying it."

She motioned to her mother, seated near the doorway, who Deidra had convinced to come to the session despite both of their fatigue.

"I have conferenced with my mother for the past two days. It's time for new leadership. I'm in charge now. And from now on we do it my way."

"You're not ready for this, Deidra," Gregor said.

Yvonne spoke up.

"She was the only one in this room who would have made the right call, the only one in this room who saw through UG deception."

"This is dangerous," Gregor replied. "Casmir is dead only three days and you're already wrenching his chair away."

Deidra's glare turned poisonous. "We need a leader now."

Yvonne broke in.

"You, of all people, know this is true, Gregor. And the council has been clear for some time that Deidra is this person. She's been part of every major decision we've made for years."

"And I've been studying Universe Three since I was six years old. I understand who we are. I understand our movement. My father is gone. My brothers are older, but we all know they couldn't handle this job even if they wanted it. If I'm *not* ready, then we're done." Deidra stood firm, holding the gazes of every person in the room as the morning breeze accented the moment.

"Beyond all that," she finally said in a low, firm voice, "I *am* the one who was right about UG's plans. I *am* the only one in this room who understood exactly who they are."

"She's right," Gregor Anderson said.

Deidra took advantage of the support to stride to the front of the stage and face her audience.

"We still have *Icarus*," she said. "And a new Star Drive will be coming off the assembly line in another month. I've spent much of the last day with Dr. Catazara and our technical staff. They're working on a wormhole breakthrough they don't think the UG has managed, at least not yet. It will take time to implement, but this war is far from over, my friends—and make no mistake that it is war. From now on we're not going to be content to sit here in the Eta Cass system. From now on we will take the thrust of the attack to them."

The council members shifted in their seats.

Deidra Francis clenched her jaw, understanding suddenly that this council was going to agree to give her power not because they agreed, but because they didn't know what else to do. A wave of disgust hit her so deeply she could barely breathe. Cowards, every one of them. She would replace them. One at a time. Person by person.

Universe Three had just changed.

That much Deidra Francis could guarantee.

The United Government had asked for a fight, and now it was going to find out just how long and just how hard Universe Three could oblige.

CHAPTER 23

Calisto Station Military Courthouse
Local Date: January 27, 2215
Local Time: 1800

"Can I have a word with you, Commander?"

Torrance had been leaving the hearing.

He looked up to see Admiral Umaro at his side and three of her staff lackeys hanging around in the background. Pages and legal aides crisscrossed the Justice Center's lobby. Lawyers and their assistants scurried around the building like sand crabs on a dry beach, talking, taking meetings, prying, and making deals. Officers strode through the hallways with brisk strides that spoke of their importance. Reporters stood in tight alcoves, hard-linked directly into their networks' reporting web.

Military police stood at attention as Ambassador Reyes came to join them.

"What do you want?" Torrance said to them both.

"Perhaps we can find a conference room," Ambassador Reyes replied.

"A place to chat would be excellent," Umaro replied, gazing around the milling public in the distance.

"Fat chance of finding a quiet place here," Torrance said.

Reyes nodded to one of his staff.

A few minutes later, the three had a small room.

The walls felt close by and were painted an off-yellow. Four padded chairs sat around an oval table made of varnished wood. A freshly vacuumed carpet absorbed their footsteps.

Reyes and Umaro took seats around the table, but Torrance just leaned against a wall.

It was very quiet.

"What's wrong?" Torrance finally said.

"I wanted to talk about your future, Torrance," Umaro said.

"Yes?" Torrance glanced at the ambassador, but Reyes betrayed no emotion.

"You present me with an interesting problem. On one hand, you're a hero. You've saved *Everguard*, and your action on *Orion* resulted in the preservation of thousands of lives on Atropos."

"Not everyone sees that as a good thing," Torrance said.

"I understand that." Umaro nodded. "So on the other hand, you're now associated with Universe Three in unpleasant ways."

"What do you mean 'associated with'?"

"Just what I said. You were responsible for destroying *Einstein*, and despite what the court just said, some people here see your act as traitorous. I'm also sure that some in Atropos City won't believe your action actually saved U3 lives. People will associate your name and image to these events, but the stories they tell will be colored by their political perspective. Positively or negatively."

"I wasn't trying to destroy a spacecraft."

"Public perception could care less about that, Torrance," the ambassador said. "But, you already know that."

"So, what are you telling me?"

Umaro leaned on the edge of the table. "We want you to consider moving away from active military."

"You mean decommission?"

He didn't like where this was going. A line of sweat built at his armpits and a warning tingle grew at the back of his neck. He stood up off the wall a bit, and went to lean on a tall chair back.

"No. Not decommission. But I think you might benefit from moving away from spacecraft operations."

"I like ops."

"I know," Umaro said. "And I know you're no conspirator, but to lead from inside Interstellar Command you will need every person you deal with to be certain of your loyalties. There are questions now. People are whispering, and the military is not without its conspiracy theorists. This aura is going to follow you now whether you want it to or not."

The truth in Umaro's words made him angry.

"Not to mention," the ambassador added, "the fact that some people are not going to be happy that the massive drain we just hit Alpha Centauri A with when *Einstein* disintegrated might well limit our ability to run Excelsior missions for a while."

Torrance gave an involuntary grimace.

The *Einstein* explosion had made a momentary rift in the wormhole connection that had fueled the ship, pulling a pure flow of fusion material into open space and adding to the drain on Alpha Centauri A. Scientists were studying the star in hopes of determining what, if any damage had been done to the link.

"I didn't mean to destroy *Einstein.*"

"And yet, you did destroy her. You were there when Universe Three attacked *Everguard.* Now you just happen to be there to toggle the targeting parameters in such a way as to destroy an Excelsior class starship."

"I didn't do that on purpose," Torrance said, clenching the back of the chair harder. "Besides, *Einstein* wasn't even our ship anymore."

"We planned to get her back, though."

Torrance looked at Admiral Umaro.

"I would never do anything to harm the Alpha Centauri A system. Actually, I was hoping to convince you to authorize a mission back there."

"Why would I do that?"

"It might be wise to measure the star's stability," he said too briskly.

Umaro gazed at Torrance with amusement that reminded him that she was fully aware of the root of his fascination with the place.

Torrance hesitated, then sighed.

"You know I've always thought we would find life on Eden, Admiral." The words were strange on his tongue this time. After all these years, to say them out loud seemed almost impossible. But there they were, out in the open.

Umaro's only reaction was to draw her lips together.

Damned anticlimactic.

"You've read Romanov's reports," Torrance said. "You know we had to delay the launch of the wormhole pods to deal with stray energy interference patterns. I believe those signals came from Eden."

"We already know the interference came from Eden."

"But they were cohesive signals."

"If that was true, Romanov would have written it."

Torrance's face grew flushed with heat. There was danger here— say too much and he could put *disobeying a commanding officer* on his record, say too little and Umaro would smell a cover-up.

"No one was sure what was going on, and Captain Romanov based his decisions on all our evidence against possible life on the planet. But I've studied the files. There is a good argument that his original interpretation could be wrong."

"I see," Umaro said, sitting back with a perplexed expression. She gazed at the ambassador.

"Actually," Reyes said. "This twist makes my proposal even more appropriate."

Torrance looked at the ambassador. "Your proposal?"

Reyes gave an over-wide grin Torrance immediately labeled as "grandfatherly."

"What the admiral hasn't told you, yet, is that I was impressed with your mindset. While the military and its culture may well find it hard to decide to trust you…given a little time on the back burner to let things cool down a little, your background makes for a good image to the public, and a good image is half my job. Your ability to develop creative solutions can make for excellent agreements. I've requested you be transferred, not retired or decommissioned."

"Excuse me?" Torrance replied.

The ambassador smiled. "I just heard you say you have an interest in alien life-forms and interstellar communities. I'm always trying to maintain a strong relationship to the scientific world, and always trying to get a better grip on how relations grow among peoples who are separated by interstellar distances. In addition, as we move forward with our explorations—which we will, of course, as a species, we are on a collision course with interstellar exploration, the only variable is time. Anyway, as I was saying, I want you to act as my primary interface with the scientific community. As we move into the future, who is to say what alien life-forms we might find." Reyes leaned forward across his crossed hands. "Who is to say what wonders you might be involved in?"

"I don't know what to say."

"I think you would say yes."

Torrance rubbed his forehead, thinking about the data. The image of Thomas Kitchell standing in the doorway of a distant office and telling Torrance he was dedicating his studies to the signals from Eden flashed through his mind.

Reyes kept speaking.

"You could be hobnobbing inside the world of scientists and extraterrestrial studies," the ambassador said with an edge to his voice that was almost excitement. "It would give you a platform to discuss your ideas in environments where they wouldn't be so controversial. And if you actually found a data-driven answer that would either support or reject your theory, you would know who to speak with about it."

"I don't know."

"It does seem perfect," the admiral said.

"What would it do to my career?"

"Nothing," Umaro said. "I would concur on the ambassador's request, and it would almost certainly be approved quickly. Actually, I think we could manage to promote you to captain with associated pay and benefits before we let you transfer. Quietly, of course. Given the situation, I don't think I'll have any problems setting that up."

The ambassador's eyes gleamed with open excitement.

It *would* be a chance to study the Eden files in ways he hadn't been able to before, and with that chance would come the ability to actually influence what happened around Alpha Centauri A.

"It's certainly interesting."

"Do I take that as a yes?" the ambassador said.

Torrance cleared his throat and took a deep breath.

"I would like to stay with Lieutenant Harthing while she goes through her convalescence."

The ambassador nodded. "That would be fine. You can go through your orientation while your friend mends."

Torrance chewed his lip.

"All right," he said. "You've got a deal."

STARCLASH

CHAPTER 24

U3 Ship *Icarus*
Local Date: Conejo 8, 9
Local Time: 1015

As Deidra took her place at the helm, Captain Keyes exited his briefing room. Seeing her, he came to her side.

"Good morning, Director."

She smiled, despite the situation at hand. She had directed both her mother and Gregor to stay behind, but all eyes were on her. Deidra knew she had to be on board for this mission. It was the first under her direction. She had chosen the target. She had worked on the structure of the mission plan. While the entire council had supported her after Gregor agreed, she felt like this mission was the litmus test. Its success or failure would make a difference. She thought of Jamal and Kel, then took a breath and cleared her mind.

"Director," she said, pronouncing the word slowly. "I remember you calling me that once before."

"I wish it were under better circumstances this time."

She pressed her lips together, but felt a sense of strength standing beside the captain. Keyes has been in her camp from the beginning.

"I feel like I can trust you, Captain."

"I appreciate hearing that."

"Are we ready?"

"Yes. All systems are tested. Skimmer missions are loaded, and bombing runs programmed. I suspect we will have twenty minutes of free time on station."

"All right."

"Do I have your permission to execute the operation?"

"Yes, Captain. Let's do it."

Keyes turned to his staff and gave the command. The bridge grew into a quiet hub as controllers focused on the jump and commanders readied their groups.

Deidra gripped the railing and scanned the profile that hung in the display straight ahead.

A map of the UG Mars Colony Natim spread out there.

She recognized the sprawling environmental control domes and the plastic tunnels that connected them up.

She remembered sitting on Perigee Hill, the highest spot on the ridge that separated the Universe Three Hive from that colony. That had been nearly a decade ago now. She remembered the sound of Papa's voice as he told her his story. Her sense of loss made her swallow hard and blink away tears that had started to form.

She wasn't going to cry.

Instead, she set her jaw and watched.

All the planning was done.

The command given.

A moment later, *Icarus* jumped from the Eta Cass system back to the Solar System.

When they arrived, the display turned to real time.

———

The first wave was a line of modified Z-pads that focused their fire on the UG police forces, which were minimal, but still capable of putting up a fight and causing problems.

The second wave, unfettered by defense, used plasma rockets and energy pulse bombs to destroy the entire agricultural wing of the colony, then doubled back and dealt with the power grid.

A final wave, Z-pads again, swooped low and targeted the community's living quarters.

"We can't do that," Gregor had argued during the planning of the mission.

"I don't recall the UG showing any restraint when they bombed the Hive," Deidra replied, highlighting the rubble that remained of what had once been their own home. "This has been a war since we bugged out. It's time we started playing like it."

The entire run lasted fifteen minutes.

When the craft returned to *Icarus*, the colony was a smoldering ruin. Deidra watched the data stream as updates came in. She pressed her lips together and ran her palms over her crossed arms, letting her sense of achievement slowly unwind from inside her, feeling a tingling that started from somewhere inside her gut, and slowly made its way up her spine until it made the skin over her shoulders crawl with a peculiar satisfaction.

The jump back to Eta Cass was perfect.

"Well done," Captain Keyes said with a crooked grin.

"Thank you," she replied. Rather than joy, Deidra felt relief. "Please give your command my appreciation."

She left, then, heading to the shuttle bay to return to Atropos City.

They hadn't lost a single spaceship.

NEWS

SOURCE: INFOWAVE — NEWS for the twenty-third century
DATE: February 2, 2215, Earth Standard
HEADLINE: U3 Attack Destroys Mars Colony Natim

UG officials announced today that a surprise attack from Universe Three resulted in the total annihilation of the Natim colony on Mars.

General Ophelia Nichols addressed the reporting pool late this evening with the news.

"The colony, known for its peaceful agricultural mission, was essentially defenseless against the onslaught, which was executed in three waves of skimmer attacks, and then a bombing pass that targeted critical life support systems."

With the United Government's acceptance, Universe Three had at one time maintained an outpost nearby the colony, a fact that most certainly allowed them to gather the intelligence they needed to complete such a surgical mission.

"Our magnanimous nature obviously worked against us," said General Nichols. "The loss is devastating."

Casualty reports include over 800 people, mostly scientists and their families.

Top United Government officials are said to be holding emergency sessions to form a response.

CHAPTER 25

Low Earth Orbit
Local Date: February 3, 2215
Local Time: 0415

Ambassador Reyes's shuttle was thirty minutes outside its reentry window. An hour after that, Torrance and Reyes would be in a conference center outside Sydney, Australia, which had been hastily chosen as the home of the emergency meeting of the Solar System Security Council. In all, it meant that Reyes had less time for pleasantries as he completed his conversation with the representative from Kensington Station.

His goal was to use the bloodlust passion the destruction of Natim had caused to kickstart a new production line.

Torrance watched his new mentor close the deal.

"That's right," Reyes said to the representative. "I think that a supporting vote from Kensington regarding prioritization of *Magellan* could result in the addition of a direct shuttle route from Kensington to

Io. At least, that's what the transportation commission has agreed to in return for other considerations."

"Then I think we have an agreement."

Reyes gave his warm smile. "It's always such a pleasure to work with you. I'll see you on the ground shortly, I hope?"

"I wouldn't miss it."

The two rang off.

"That was impressive," Torrance said. "I didn't think a direct route to Io would make that much of a difference to her."

Reyes raised one eyebrow and cocked his head. "This is why relationships matter, Torrance. Kensington's representative and I have been making arrangements for years, and through most of that time I've been giving her the larger end of the stick. But this is the most important. She understands that, so she's letting me win on the face of it. But she also understands that her people are angry and looking for revenge. They won't mind the appearance of an overpay. In fact, an overpay is a sign of courage. If, later though, she can claim to be the source of the Io route, that will be helpful to her. And regardless she can both lay claim to the extra commerce made through it, as well as direct that commerce stream to places of her choosing."

Reyes hesitated, looking at the display that showed the shuttle's progress.

"And there are also other advantages to be had in developing a new trade route," he finally said.

"Such as?"

"Such as the fact that there are shipping licenses that have to be approved, extra facilities to be built and regulated, people to be hired to run it all."

Torrance's face lit up. "And she who controls the build, controls the votes that come with the build."

Reyes patted him high on the shoulder. "See what I mean? You are already proving my intuition to be good."

Torrance grinned.

He wasn't sure how he felt about what he had witnessed over the past several hours of the flight.

Reyes had been on the communicator the whole time.

During a call with the vice mayor of Venus Station, Reyes agreed that it would be a good thing to change the current division of the automated mining rights to the olivine that lay under that planet's crust, which was packaged for use in CO_2 scrubbers around the system. That re-division would, of course, come with a need to alter the district voting lines, which was only prudent. In the meantime, Venus Station also agreed that the science-oriented *Magellan* spacecraft's build should be prioritized third on the list, after the initial two battle cruisers that would be needed for defense.

Reyes had also held a conference with a financier on Europa, who offered to open an entirely new production line to build *Magellan*, which was an obvious value because it would mean the prioritization was merely about adding additional money rather than diverting resources from the existing buildup toward war with U3.

All total, Ambassador Reyes had introduced Torrance to twelve of the Solar System's more powerful people in the past eight hours.

"What are you thinking?" Reyes said.

"I'm not sure."

Reyes gave a sage nod.

"Negotiations are like impressionistic paintings, Torrance."

"How so?"

"They are rarely pristine when you look at them up close. In fact, the closer you are to the details, sometimes the less obvious it is what you're doing. But the goal is always to be thinking about how it looks when you step back."

"Mostly it just feels like giving everyone something in order to get what you want."

"Yes, yes. But there is an art to that. You see it, right? Everyone gets what they want, and still you move civilization as we know it forward."

Torrance picked up the empty teacup in front of him, then put it down.

"When we all vote to accelerate and redistribute the build of more Star Drives, the supreme president gets to look strong," Torrance said. "And the people get to feel like they are doing something noble because they think the politicians are protecting them."

"That's because those politicians *are* protecting them."

"Are they?"

"Yes."

"Because what I see are a group of business people who are really just gathering stronger control of their public."

"Yes," Reyes responded. "They are. But they are also protecting the people."

Torrance understood that. If "the people" were willing to give up economic freedom for protection, he supposed that was their right.

"What do we get?"

"Who is we?"

"The rest of the people," Torrance responded. "People who don't want to be manipulated like that."

"Ah," Reyes asked. "You mean, the dreamers?"

"Sure."

"Well, if we do our jobs right, the people like that get *Magellan* earlier than they would have otherwise."

Torrance nodded.

Magellan was the new Star Drive spacecraft that would take scientists and engineers to the stars. If Reyes got his way, the group in Io would begin building *Magellan* soon, if nothing else to act as a trial run to discover what it took to open another assembly line. More spacecraft would be built in several other jurisdictions, of course, an arrangement Reyes had almost completed cementing, and a process that would gain credibility if he could get the votes later today.

Torrance thought about Thomas Kitchell.

Magellan would be a perfect ship for a man like Kitchell to establish his career.

"I see," Torrance said.

"That's good."

Reyes looked at the system time.

Abke's voice came over the intercom: Five minutes to reentry stations.

"I think we should get ourselves ready," Reyes said.

CHAPTER 26

Atropos, Eta Cassiopeia System
Local Date: Conejo 10, 9
Local Time: 0915

"Are you sure this is wise?"

Kazima Yamada, a supporter of Deidra's father, was in her forties now and of no little sway within the council. She had asked for time with Deidra prior to the next joint planning session, obviously with the intention of providing her own guidance. Yamada's coordination of the engineering efforts around the colony had made major inroads, but she was a person of a million ideas, and now that they were walking together outside the Castle, Deidra took her in with a sidewise glance. She hadn't considered Yamada a competitor for the directorship, but even now, after the smashing success of the Natim operation, it was possible Kazima Yamada could attempt a soft coup of sorts.

The morning was pleasant enough, Eta Cass had risen earlier, and the temperature was still cool. A breeze pushed the two women's hair across their faces, and carried the smell of spring flowers and the sounds of the morning work crews constructing more of the endless buildings and roads that the city needed to construct as it grew. The weather had been clear for the past several days, but now a collection of clouds threatened to roll over the city from the west. Reports called for rain later tonight.

"We've destroyed Natim," Yamada said. "Do we really need to go back to Miranda Station?"

"The destruction of Natim is not enough," Deidra replied. "The first raid was a statement, the next is a strategic imperative."

"I'm not sure your father would—"

"My father has nothing to do with this."

"Are you sure of that?"

"Has anything changed about the UG's ability to outpace our production rates?"

"No," Yamada replied.

"And has anything changed about the criticality of this moment?"

"The reaction of the people isn't available yet."

Yamada was referring to the reconnaissance jump that *Icarus* was in the process of running now—jumping back to the Solar System in a few key "safe zones" in order to gather the public news broadcasts that would give Universe Three's council a read on how the population was feeling.

"I think it's best to assume the worst."

"Your father—"

Deidra came to an abrupt halt.

"My father is not here, Kazima," she said. "If you think anyone is more aware of that fact than I am, you're sadly mistaken. But the fact is that my father's approach is what got him killed. Papa ignored the obvious because he got too close to his dream and let his guard down. The difference between me and the rest of the council is that I am not afraid to say that. And the next fact here is that the people of the Solar System are mostly sheep, just like Ellyn Parker said they were. I don't need the publicity report to predict that the majority of them will rise up to fight us because that is exactly what they've been conditioned to do."

"There will be some, though—"

"And those few we will find a way to help."

Yamada nodded her agreement.

What else was Yamada supposed to do, though, Deidra wondered. Deidra wanted to trust the engineer because, despite her questioning approach, Yamada had been one of her father's closer confidants. But right now Deidra was struggling to separate the truth from her natural paranoia. Though Jamal hadn't meant to comment on her situation, he had said it well last night when she returned home and couldn't calm down. "I don't suppose anyone's getting any sleep tonight," he said. Of course, he said it as Kel was snoring away, which made perfect sense at the time. The whole thing was hard to make anything of. She was trying to put one step in front of the next, and trying to make sure everything pointed in the right direction.

Deidra looked at Yamada.

"I'm sorry to be so abrupt, Kazima," she said.

"It's all right," Yamada replied. "It's a sensitive time. Everyone is on edge."

"Sensitive or not, we still have a problem." Deidra felt better just voicing it. "Now more than ever, we have to stop the United Government from building Star Drive craft or they will get the upper hand. We all agreed with that much, earlier. And the key to that has always been Miranda Station."

"We could choose the less risky option."

Yamada was referring to Gregor Anderson's scheme wherein U3 would jump *Icarus* to a series of locations in a single sweep, breaking the UG production flow by removing at least four key components— the primary one being an exotic matter containment plant that was hidden in plain sight on Tethys, an inner moon of Saturn, a placement made practical due to the moon's proximity to sources of titanium and iron ores in the Saturn ring moonlets and the massive amounts of hydrogen stored in the form of the water that made up most of Tethys's actual body. Destroy the sources, said the idea, and you destroy the ability to build.

"That would be more dangerous now," Deidra said.

"Why do you say that?"

"Because," Deidra said, hesitating a moment to consider how forthright she should be, then deciding to go ahead. This would be a test, she thought. A test of just how Kazima Yamada might relate with her —if not quite a measure of trustworthiness, at least her reaction could give Deidra an idea of how loyal Yamada might be. "We left trails behind that pointed to Gregor's scheme."

A frown crossed Yamada's face at first, but it was more of an inquisitive expression than one of displeasure. Then it lightened to an expression that wasn't quite a smile, but was perhaps more one of admiration.

"I see," she said. "That was risky."

"We needed a diversion."

"The council probably wouldn't have approved it."

"Our ability to be nimble is our only advantage, Kazima. We can't win by running everything through the council."

Yamada's expression became a full smile then. "You are definitely your father's daughter," she said.

"You'll support me, then?"

Yamada nodded. She ran her hand through her hair after the breeze picked it up again. "Yes," she said. "Given that, I think Miranda Station is the place."

Deidra breathed a sigh of relief.

It was good to know she had Yamada's support.

CHAPTER 27

Sidney, Australia
Local Date: February 3, 2215
Local Time: 0615

Willim Pinot, manager of the Interstellar Insurgency branch of the UG Intelligence Office, scanned the display as he walked on his treadmill. He was tall, and his gait was still the same awkward motion it had been when he was younger. His knees ached now, though. Not good for someone who wasn't yet officially old.

An insulated coffee mug sat in the holder to his right.

A plush, golden towel draped over his shoulders.

Outside the twenty-fifth-floor hotel exercise room, the sun rose out of the Pacific Ocean. An hour from now he would be gathering with several hundred other people—leaders of every faction in the Solar System's governmental structure, and their entourages, of course—in the hotel's basement conference center, a large meeting hall outfitted with both physical and virtual stations.

They would be voting on an proclamation to officially make the production of additional Excelsior class Star Drive systems the highest priority on all agendas. It was a sham vote, of course. There was no political drive to do anything else, and actions were already being taken as if the directive was signed. So the session would mostly be about leaders making preconfigured speeches that played to their constituents, as if that really mattered—which, he supposed it did, really. The idea that people still had a choice in who led them was vital to manage unless one was interested in an uprising.

Pinot, however, was here for a different game.

He thought about that as he pushed the velocity on the treadmill up to five kph.

His official reason for being here was to support his boss, Sela Matz, who was still the system's Chief Intelligence Officer. While it wasn't openly discussed, Pinot knew Matz was going to leave her post soon. Some said Supreme President Laney Mubadid had asked Matz to help in her reelection efforts, others thought Matz was being pressured to run for the position herself—which was a stupid idea in the end. No spook leader stood a real chance of beating a corporate leader, and Pinot knew his boss to be smart enough to understand that.

Regardless, it meant the CIO position was going to be open, and Pinot was here to stake his claim.

And now, more than ever, that would mean being right about Universe Three.

More reports from the Natim raid were coming in.

He smiled as he scanned them.

With Casmir Francis dead, the rest of the intelligence community was busy determining who was in charge of the terroristic group. The general consensus leaned to the Number Two man, Gregor Anderson. That would be the standard play. Anderson had been part of the U3 power structure for a long time, and the transition would be smooth. It was natural to think U3 would simply move their second in command up to fill the leadership role of their dead martyr.

Pinot's team analyzed the stream of bits that had come into UG receivers, small snippets of communication that had passed between Universe Three raiders as they completed the mission. One mentioned

Aldrin Station, which is near where *Everguard* had been scuttled. Another spoke of Kensington Station, a key element of the mining operation that fed the Excelsior manufacturing capacity. Two separate items mentioned Tethys, which was interesting because of the exotic matter containment plant located there.

Together, his team had decided they were possible points of the next raid.

And if Gregor Anderson was the man in charge, perhaps they would be right. Anderson had a straightforward sensibility to him. Anderson wouldn't play a game of feints and dodges before reaching for the UG's gonads.

But Pinot had studied Anderson as fully as he had studied Francis, and the bottom line was that the Natim operation wasn't in the man's playbook.

In retrospect *Icarus*'s arrival point was the first domino to fall for Pinot. The Universe Three spacecraft had entered Mars orbit in the exact coordinates relative to the planet that the UG had jumped *Orion* to in order to launch the attack on U3's outpost all those years ago. He had noted it then, but hadn't put the whole thing together until later.

Now, every report that came in included a tidbit of information that filled in the gaps as certainly as if they were mortar being used to lay bricks.

Just as *Icarus*'s launch coordinates were precisely placed, the flight paths had been sublimely coordinated. The battle order—U3's work to strip gun placements first—was a familiar callout to that first assault, too, and the drop pattern of the bombing runs had been matched as perfectly as they could have been matched to the UG raid.

He smiled as he took in the entire work.

The whole of the plan told him what he needed to know.

This operation had been a piece of art.

It was about revenge, yes, but a special kind of revenge.

Specific. Pointed.

This was an attack that meant something personal to whoever laid it out, and that alone led him to one person.

Deidra Francis was in charge now.

And Deidra Francis was a different beast altogether.

Pinot stopped the treadmill, wiped a bead of sweat from his brow, and went to the shower room to prepare.

Life in this little nook of the galaxy was about to get interesting.

———

Pinot was a touch late getting to his seat, so the representative from Calisto was already on the floor giving a fiery speech in which he promised the peaceful people of his station were not willing to let Universe Three get away with this atrocity, and pledged to take any steps necessary to see them come to justice.

Pinot nodded to his boss, who was, as always, seated in a position that gave her access to see the entire room with the exception of the few seats that had been reserved for her people.

Her nod on his arrival said she had received his notice.

The tilt of her head said she wanted to discuss it.

He took the open seat beside her.

"Your team says Universe Three will strike Kensington," she said to him while keeping her gaze on Calisto's representative.

"Yes," Pinot replied while keeping a similar posture. "That's what they say."

"It's unusual for a leader to argue against his own team."

Pinot ran his fingers down the sides of his thin goatee. He understood her comment—leaders who went against the grain of their own organization ran certain risks no matter what happened, different risks depending on if they were right or wrong, but risks. It was easier to take the advice of others, and then sidestep blame if that advice wound up wrong.

"You know me, Sela," Pinot replied.

Her grin was cold.

"Yes," she said. "I do."

"She gave us those snippets on purpose."

"She?"

"Deidra Francis."

Matz's eyes closed slightly as she considered his inference.

"Universe Three will go back to Miranda Station," Pinot said as she thought. "It's all in the brief I sent you. She'll attempt to cut the head off our program right now. I can even give you the plan she'll use."

"If this is wrong, we're both done."

"It's not wrong."

As the silence grew, Pinot felt the strength of that statement also grow. He was right. He had to be right. Such certainty is dangerous to a person of his profession. Certainty in the eye of probability is the first step to false ideology. But now that he had said it out loud, the sensation of certainty fell over him like a warm shower.

"Get me on Admiral Umaro's calendar," Matz finally said. Then she sat back and listened impassively as the representative of Calisto gave the floor to the representative from Europa Colony Davies.

Pinot pressed his lips into a single line, rose from his chair, and left the room. He had won. There was only one reason to call on Umaro. His boss was a person who knew how to push buttons, and now she was going to push Admiral Umaro's buttons.

Orion was going to be deployed to Miranda Station.

CHAPTER 28

Sidney, Australia
Local Date: February 3, 2215
Local Time: 0815

From across the conference hall, Torrance watched the tall man pick his way to a seat beside the UG's Chief Intelligence Officer. He should know who this man was, he thought. Reyes had been pushing him to learn all the administrators of all the major factions in the UG hierarchy by sight, but there was so much to learn in so much time. He knew Sela Matz was the CIO, but he came up blank on the man.

He watched them speak, though.

It felt unreal. Like he was watching a spy movie.

After a few minutes, the man got up and left the room.

"Did you see that?" Reyes said when it was obvious Torrance had. "Willim Pinot," the ambassador added.

"Thank you."

"When you come to these, you watch everything," Reyes said. "There are games being played everywhere."

"What game was that?"

The shoulders of Reyes's ambassadorial robes rose in a shrug.

"The games played by intelligence agents are rarely clear, Torrance, but the right question to always ask is what is it that they want."

Torrance took in that idea.

What did the CIO want here?

What game was Pinot playing?

What would the intelligence community get from a decision on how to accelerate building the Excelsior spacecraft or the decision on where to put the additional production capabilities?

"Are they worried about losing funding?"

Reyes puckered his lips and shook his head no. "Most of their money is black, anyway. Not even the supreme president knows what the intelligence community actually spends."

Torrance thought harder.

The intelligence community didn't really have a play here, did it? Sela Matz had no vote in the decision. She wasn't lobbying anyone.

"Why would the intelligence community even be here?" he said.

"That's another good way to phrase the question."

Torrance took a breath and scanned the entire room, noting how Sela Matz was doing the same thing. He watched her work, watched the men and women who sat in her area work—because that's what they were doing, working, watching and absorbing, taking in behaviors, making notes. As he scanned the room, the CIO's dark brown gaze locked directly with his.

His breakfast turned sour in his belly, and he suddenly felt the same chill that he had felt when he first stepped into Government Security Officer Casey's office on *Everguard*.

On the floor, the leader from Io asked his compatriots to add a new production line to enhance scientific research. "Vote yes on the military," he called out, "but let's add more, vote yes on the brave adventurers we have in our midst, too. Vote, yes," he said amid light applause. "I say vote yes, and yes, and yes."

———

A grueling six hours later, the resolution passed with only three nays and four abstentions. The bill included an immediate spending increase for the defense of all existing manufacturing facilities that supported the Star Drive program, and military support for all space stations, corporations, direct contractors, and suppliers that touched on the manufacturing pipeline.

"We will also be putting key science personnel under lockdown to protect them from harm," added General Ophelia Nichols, who was announced as the new UG press secretary, responsible for all information regarding the action that was now officially being considered as the first interstellar war in history.

As far as Torrance could tell, the spending bill had no defined cap. Not that it mattered.

As he left the conference hall, Torrance thought about the ruins of Mars Colony Natim, some of which was reported to still be burning. He remembered *Everguard*.

He wasn't going to lie to himself and pretend that the escalation he had seen in the past few weeks didn't leave him unnerved, but as he watched the show unfold before him a certain essence of resolved understanding came over him. What else was there to do, after all? The UG had tried peace, and its own military had intervened. Universe Three was most unlikely to agree to another parlay.

Still, Torrance was also not going to deny the sense of hopeless dread that crept over him, a feeling accompanied by a touch of help-lessness.

Even if he could see a different way out, which he couldn't, Torrance felt the unstoppable wheels of power moving now.

The blood in the room was up, and that gave everything a sensa-tion of being out of control that he didn't like. Torrance understood reason. He understood cause and effect. This was what made him good at what he did. But sitting here amid this discussion, watching the speakers parade up to the podium and watching the security and intelligence officers in the room work, Torrance felt the world shifting underneath him.

When the meeting had started, the United Government was not expected to launch their next Excelsior class ship for as many as nine months, but now he was sure that date would be considerably sooner.

That was good, wasn't it?

CHAPTER 29

U3 Ship *Icarus*, Pod Bay
Local Date: Conejo 14, 9
Local Time: 1320

Matt Anderson had run this mission before, though they were approaching from the west and north this time, rather than the east, and this time he had an entire squadron of combatants under his command rather than just two. Intel suggested a new ring of plasma cannons had been placed on Miranda herself, and their mole was assigned to bunker three, positioned in the northern hemisphere.

Anderson sat in his Z-pad, waiting for the jump to finish, wondering about the mole.

It was a dangerous life, infiltrating the UG and feeding information back. Intense. He wouldn't want to do that kind of work, live that kind of life. Certain identities were kept quiet, but the rumor was that the average lifespan of a U3 spy was no better than a few years at best. This one, whoever it was, would be running a tight line. He or she was going to take down the bunker from within, allowing the mission to proceed more quickly and effectively than it would have if Z-pad cover had to be peeled off to destroy the cannon before the rest of the mission could proceed.

A voice came through his headset.

"Jump target achieved in five…four…"

He scanned the control panels, and saw the mission plan was scrolling.

"Three…two…"

They had forty minutes from bay door open to return. Anything more than that would give UG's *Orion* time to jump in and disrupt the cycle. *Icarus* would arrive, the doors would open, and then they had five minutes to shoot the gap to Miranda's horizon, ten minutes on station to destroy as much of the thing that they could destroy. That was the good thing—they weren't here to gather up anything, only to destroy. The mission had patterns planned, but everyone knows that a full-scale battle like this wasn't something that played to plan. At the end of the day, he was going hunting, and that was fine by him.

UG had killed Casmir Francis like the cowards they were.

He gripped his yoke.

"One…"

He swallowed hard. The rumbling of the engines shook the entire craft as its engines spun up.

"On zone."

The doors began to open. Light from the edge of the moon illuminated the dark Z-pad bay.

"Go mission," the voice said.

Acceleration pressed Anderson into his seat as the Z-pad launched, then released. His squadron formed up as it streamed toward the horizon.

The sensor screen began to scream at him and flash yellow. "Intruders locked," the system told him.

Intruders.

He gritted his teeth and twisted the yoke to make an avoiding roll. A plasma rocket flashed past. Another Z-pad exploded at the depths of his periphery.

He saw UG skimmercraft homing in on him, and homing in on *Icarus* herself. He was going to be too late. He saw that, then. The attack force was intense—too intense to mean anything except that *Orion* had been stationed here. None of the Z-pads would make it back before *Icarus* was destroyed. If she stayed on station, everything was lost.

"Abort!" he called into the communicator, and stomped on the deflector to put his skimmer into an inside loop that would bring him around. "The bastards knew we were coming!"

He didn't see the UG skimmer on his left, but his sensor screen alerted him, and his threat analysis system adjusted his course. He put himself into a wide barrel roll, focusing his sight on a single bright star in the middle of the velvety black patch of deep space that filled the view outside his cockpit.

That darkness and that star were the last things Matt Anderson saw.

In the distance, *Icarus* shut its pod bay doors, and, as Z-pads exploded into fragments, jumped its way out of the Solar System.

NEWS

SOURCE: INFOWAVE — NEWS for the twenty-third century
DATE: February 6, 2215, Earth Standard
HEADLINE: Universe Three Attack Thwarted

With news of the attack on Mars Colony Natim still fresh on everyone's minds, word that UG forces have repelled a second such operation comes as revitalizing news. Officials announced that a sortie of U3 Z-pad fighters had been intercepted prior to their arrival on site at Miranda Station.

"We stopped them cold," said Press Secretary Ophelia Nichols.

She went on to suggest that the rapid-fire attacks coming from Universe Three suggest that the terrorist organization is worried they will fall behind UG's production capability.

"I would worry if I were them, too," she said.

When asked if Interstellar Command had plans to take the attack to the U3 bases in Eta Cassiopeia, Nichols had no direct answer.

"It is our policy not to discuss possible actions so as to protect our brave fighting citizens."

CHAPTER 30

Sidney, Australia
Local Date: February 6, 2215
Local Time: 2230

Torrance Black sat under a cloudless nighttime sky on the balcony of his hotel suite, thinking about the events of the day and the news about the successful defense of Miranda Station. From this height, the lights of the coastline created an artificial rim ringing the pitch-black of the water. The lights of boats and ships moved with artificial grace out in the ocean's currents, which seemed an appropriate metaphor for the past three days. They all seemed to be heading somewhere specific, and all seemed to move with a practiced smoothness, but Torrance knew that everything would be different if he was standing on the deck of any of those ships.

Ambassador Reyes sat across the table.

The breeze was warm and carried the scent of the water.

Remnants of their room service dinner were littered across the table. Reyes gave a liberal pour of a third glass of wine. Torrance cracked what would be his last beer of the evening.

He was dead tired.

Reyes looked tired, too, the lines of his face creating shadowed crevasses in the angled lighting of the balcony. But while the ambassador appeared to be basking in the fatigue of achievement—which Torrance thought was probably fair seeing as Reyes had managed to get his extra manufacturing line approved in the chaos of the other votes—Torrance merely felt anxious.

"I don't think this is working," Torrance said.

"What do you mean?"

"I don't know what I'm supposed to be doing here."

Reyes sipped his wine and gave a smile that spoke of gentle satisfaction. "Tell me more."

"I don't see how I'm helping."

"You're helping by learning how things work—which is what a good engineer does, right? Learns how things work?"

"Sure, but…" Torrance hesitated. Looked out into the darkness, and sipped his own drink. The beer was sharp and bit into the back of his throat as he swallowed. "I don't know."

"You're asking yourself what you can accomplish here, is that it?"

"Sure."

"You're thinking that in the old days you had a problem and if you twisted the right screwdriver or flipped the right bit, that problem would go away."

"That's a seriously simple way to look at it."

"Is it?"

"Keeping a shipboard system running is a lot more complicated than turning a screwdriver and flipping a switch."

"Kind of like getting your way in a debate?"

Torrance laughed, then drank again. He had been starving before they ate, and the sensation of being full was catching up to him. "What's your point?"

"At the end of the day, Torrance, working with people is not really much different from working with a piece of technology. And, in truth, it's probably even more simple."

"That's not true."

"Sure it is."

"People don't have equations."

"Now *that* is actually what is not true. People are among the most predictable systems in the universe. You just have to study them awhile, and be okay with classifying them in ways that make sense."

Torrance rolled his eyes.

"I'm serious." He put his wineglass down. "I find that the people who have the most problems dealing with other people are the ones who are afraid to make judgments. They don't want to think badly of another person, so they try to figure out why that person is behaving in ways they don't understand."

"I don't think the problem is that I'm not judgmental."

"Sure it is."

Torrance chuckled. "Tell that to my ex-wife."

"Universe Three is doing exactly what the United Government would do if the positions were reversed, for example," Reyes continued. "And the UG is doing exactly what U3 would be doing. The methods and reactions are the same because we are all human beings."

"You're saying war is inevitable. That we have to just sit back and watch it happen?"

"Not inevitable, but likely. The history of humankind is really told in its wars, right?" Torrance grunted a reply, so Reyes went on. "In fact, I posit that you can tell a lot about how people work by studying the actual causes of war."

Torrance examined the ambassador.

The man was relaxed now, comfortable for the first time since they had arrived.

"I guess you're right."

"What are you really worried about?" Reyes said.

"I don't know if I can make a difference anymore."

Torrance stopped himself there. This was the first time he had said that. "The world is too big. Things move on their own, and there's no way we can stop them."

Reyes picked up the plate that held the remaining crumbs of his dessert, used a fork to press out the last bit, then ate it. He put the plate down, then sat back.

"Every war is changed by individuals, Torrance. Every decision is made by a person and executed by a person."

"You're saying we can stop this?"

"I'm saying you can make a difference. I'm saying that to make a difference in times of conflict a person has to make decisions—judgments, some of them unpleasant—and then you have to actually do something. I'm saying you can't make a difference when you're sitting on the sideline. You, of all people, should understand that."

Torrance shook his head.

"I was hoping you would make a difference on Europa, actually," Reyes said, his voice suddenly quite direct.

"Europa?"

"I think it would be useful to have a UG ambassador in the facility that is responsible for building *Magellan*."

"You want me to work with *Magellan*?"

"It would be a good way to make a difference."

Torrance took a breath of the ocean air and rubbed his eyes. Yes, he was tired, and yes, it seemed like war was going to happen no matter what he did. But now that *Magellan* was on the build slate, yes, maybe there was some kind of hope.

"We could also arrange to have Lieutenant Harthing brought there to complete her convalescence."

Torrance smiled.

"What would I have to do?"

Reyes smiled, and sipped his wine. "Well, probably move to Europa for starters."

CHAPTER 31

Atropos, Eta Cassiopeia System
Local Date: Conejo 14, 9
Local Time: 1515

Deidra sat in the navigation control room with several other planners, specifically including her mentor, Katriana Martinez. She was trying to remain calm, trying to be collected and confident, as she had seen her father be in these situations—situations where there was nothing left for her to do. It was harder from the inside than it appeared on the outside.

Her anxiety was the reason she came here. This room felt comfortable to her, more comfortable than any other place except the woods and lakebed, really. She had been involved in most aspects of U3's management systems since she was quite young, but she had always felt that her official start came in navigation.

As with every return jump, *Icarus* came onto the grid as a tiny electronic blip, followed by the projector converting it to a green symbol that hovered in low orbit around the map of the planet that served as the mission's overall status report. Everyone in the control room saw it, including Deidra and including Katriana Martinez. This was the standard return point, a reference that Katriana had developed when she realized that a standard receiving location would force a systematic planning process—Deidra appreciated that about Katriana. She liked things to be standard.

What wasn't standard, though, was the timing of *Icarus*'s arrival. It was a full hour ahead of schedule, a timing that spoke volumes.

The voice of Captain Keyes came over the speaker. "Operation Miranda Three was shut down two minutes in," he said. "Full details to follow."

When the comm officer reported the rest of the news, faces grew past dark and onto morbid.

The mission was a disaster.

Though she could still jump, *Icarus* was damaged.

Thirty-five Z-pad skimmers were gone.

Deidra's first reaction was to bite down a need to scream. Her heart raced, and a chill emanated from her chest to travel down her arms and legs.

"We need to contact Vice Director Anderson," Katriana said after absorbing what this meant. "As well as the others who have lost people."

A communications worker started to get a link to Anderson's system.

"No," Katriana said, stopping him.

She put her hand on Deidra's shoulder. "A parent shouldn't be alone when he hears of the loss of his child."

The hurt that still flavored Katriana's expression hit Deidra like a wave of stale water on top of the anger that was boiling inside her. Katriana understood loss.

They locked gazes for what seemed a half a beat too long, but with a power that gave Deidra a moment to breathe.

Deidra nodded. "I'll go tell him."

As she stood, the projection image flickered, and a red blip appeared in orbit above Atropos City.

"Foreign presence detected," the operator called.

Deidra whirled to take in the image, then glanced at Katriana, who frowned and shook her head in uncertainty. Additional images appeared to separate from the central red blotch.

"Skimmers," Katriana finally said.

"It's *Orion*," Deidra replied. A chill of dread came over her. If this wasn't such a dire situation, she would be impressed at the audacity of the response. How unlike the UG to be so nimble. "Call a warning. Battle stations. Tell Keyes to launch any interceptors he's got."

"The UG," Katriana said.

"The bastards followed us. They knew we were coming. They hit us, then they followed us back."

———

The first explosion came less than a minute later.

Deidra grabbed a guard's laser rifle, and ran out to the street.

A plant that made basic machinery went up in flames as a skimmer flashed by overhead. A second and third craft made passes at the central road that ran through the city. A marketplace was blazing, billowing clouds of black smoke rising into the afternoon sky. The air was full of UG skimmers, flying nearly unabated, dropping ordinance and laser fire down in wide swaths. The ground shook from explosions around the city. In moments, smoke rose from several places across the horizon.

She aimed at a skimmer and pressed off a shot that missed.

A scream came to her voice then, a long, drawn-out wail that got covered up by explosions and the whine of skimmer engines. She wanted to slice the laser through the sky, but this was a small weapon designed for close combat—its projectile was a concentrated pulse rather than a slicing beam. She shot again, and again, targeting craft that moved too fast to hit.

She ran to the middle of a street crossing, firing into the air, hoping her laser fire was a beacon.

It worked.

A UG skimmer turned on its run, and approached her head-on.

She raised the laser to her shoulder, took direct aim at the onrushing profile, and squeezed off a shot.

Just as the skimmer opened fire on her.

She rolled away.

An explosion loud enough to rattle her skull came from behind her, around her, under her, through her. The ground welled up in cracked chunks that flew through the air. A wave of heat seemed to scour her skin.

Then everything went silent.

Deidra raised herself up, digging out of dirt and debris, fighting the pain in her elbow and the way her arm dangled at an awkward angle when she could finally stand. She looked for the rifle, but it was gone, tossed somewhere in the blast. The ground around her smoldered, and the crumbled remains of the skimmer she had shot from the sky lay scattered on a path that started nearby and seemed to go on forever.

The sky was marred by ugly fire, but it was empty of skimmers.

The UG had hit, then collected their craft and gotten out of the region before they could lose much.

She gritted her teeth against the anger that welled in her chest.

"Deidra!"

She turned to see Katriana Martinez rushing through the rubble.

"Thank God, you're alive," Katriana said as she drew near. "But, your arm!"

When Katriana said it, Deidra's arm began to throb. She groaned with the pain.

"I was so stupid!" Deidra said, panting through the pain and blinking back tears that came from so much more. She fell to her knees and screamed.

Katriana came to her side. "We've got to get that arm set."

"This is who they are," Deidra spat. "I've known that. Give the UG any form of superiority, and they will always move to crush resistance. I should have known this. I should have…they killed Ellyn Parker, they killed our people across the Solar System at any chance they had. They had attacked us in our first days. They killed my father, and now they've killed Matt Anderson and who knows how many more?"

Katriana put her arm around Deidra's shoulder to pull her closer. The warmth of her body felt good.

"They will pay for this," Katriana said. "Right?"

Deidra nodded, tasting sweat and dirt at the corners of her mouth.

"Yes," she said. "They will pay for this."

CHAPTER 32

Chicago, Illinois
Local Date: February 13, 2215
Local Time: 0845

"Are you available?"

The message hung at the corner of Willim Pinot's desk. It was from Sela Matz. Even if it hadn't come with her label attached, he would have known it was from her due to the direct nature of its wording. Other people would have added more: *Are you available to talk?* or *Are you available for a coffee?* Or they would have taken a more indirect approach like *Do you have any time today?*

But Sela Matz, as marvelously detailed as her operations could be, had never been indirect about these kinds of things.

"Yes," he replied.

There was no reply. Not that there needed to be.

Pinot cleared his projection system of his notes and the brief he had been working through. He had fifteen agents working for him now, and each filed several reports a day on subjects that ranged from the actions of known Universe Three sympathizers, to projections on the effects of Operation Yo-yo, the retaliation raid on Atropos City.

Then he sat back, considering the situation.

The lack of response meant Matz was coming to his office, which was a detail that mattered. There were several reasons his boss could be choosing to come to him rather than call him to her, specifically including the idea that she preferred their conversation to be free of any possible leaks that could occur if it were held in her own office. Then, of course, one would have to weigh these risks against possible leaks coming from his own office—of which he was sure there were some. One of the things he liked most about the spook game was that intelligence work was mostly about the anti-game, managing disinformation.

You work your ass off to shut down leaks, but when you find one the first question is not about shutting it down, but instead whether you can use the source to feed the enemy information that diverted them from your real purposes.

And then, could you use them to create even more intricate operations.

To Willim Pinot, his job was a form of art. The webs could be beautiful in their entanglements.

Ten minutes later, Sela Matz arrived at his office.

"Good morning," she said as she sat down.

She was wearing a sharp outfit, a pressed, simple blouse of dark green over a pair of professionally creased beige pants. She wore no jewelry, but her comm button was in one ear. Her hair was, as always, in perfect place despite her walk over.

"Good morning," Pinot replied. "To what do I owe the pleasure?"

"The supreme president has given me her appreciation for the work that went into planning Yo-yo."

"That's good to hear."

"When I told her it was mostly your work, she asked me to pass them on to you personally."

"Thank you."

"Along with her request that you consider taking my position."

Pinot smiled, as he assumed he was supposed to.

"I assume you're aware that she has asked me to take a more direct advisory role in her administration."

"It was among possibilities I had understood," Pinot said.

"I gave her your name as my replacement."

"I'm honored."

Matz sat still in the chair. Her expression seemed to condense into a single focus, and she edged forward as Pinot watched her.

"Cut the bullshit, Willim," she said. "That kind of act is great for everyone else, but we both know you want the job and we both know that you've had your fingers on what was happening with me. I would have recommended you anyway, but saving Miranda and hitting back with Yo-yo was the key that unlocked the door as far as Laney was concerned."

"I like working with you, Sela. Thank you."

Matz's relaxation was just enough to be noticeable. "Here's the deal, Willim. I want us to always be straight. No bullshit from this point on. You take this office, you're in charge. You take it and we rely on each other."

"You'll give me a feed on Mubadid's action?"

"And anything else on the cabinet that seems to make sense."

"And I give you ops info."

"And intel on activists who gather too much power or make too much noise—preferably before they get to be a real problem."

"Of course," Pinot said. "The government that runs best is the government that greases the skids."

"Exactly," Matz replied. "Together, we can be the grease."

Pinot took a deep breath and sat back in his chair. They both knew that last statement was too simple. In the game of politics, applying grease had a way of actually changing the skids. There was no reason to voice this, though. No reason to say aloud that in this configuration Sela Matz and Willim Pinot alone could conspire to change civilization in ways they felt was for the better, that control of information was the most important force in existence, and that in this configuration the two of them could be the two most powerful people in the Solar System.

And the fact of the matter was that in this configuration, Willim Pinot was the more powerful of the two.

Yes, Matz could give him simple access to information and people he couldn't easily get elsewhere, but he could control everything that the leadership of the United Government heard whether it was true or not.

This was it, he thought. This was his dream.

He was sure there would be a process—meetings, hearings, confirmations. But he understood how this game was played. If the supreme president wanted it to happen, it would happen. And Sela Matz would ensure the supreme president wanted it to happen. Beyond the facts of their past relationship, which had always been professional and productive, he knew she had his back because she had come here, rather than summon him to her place. Coming here was a vote of confidence in itself. It said it was his job to deal with the internal fallout. Coming here gave him control of the message, and said she knew he could deal with any fallout.

That realization built a sense of victory that made him feel like he was going to combust there on the spot.

He was one person, yes. But he was about to become one person who could shape the rest of the world.

"That sounds fantastic," he finally said. "I can't wait to help."

CHAPTER 33

Atropos, Eta Cassiopeia System
Local Date: Conejo 14, 9
Local Time: 1730

Gregor Anderson's living quarters was a standard mudbrick house built on a solid foundation. It consisted of six rooms, including the small kitchen.

Paying extreme attention to her disheveled appearance and her broken arm, which Dr. Iwal had already set and put into a sling, Gregor's aide let Deidra directly into the study.

A small computing pad sat on one side of the desk, a cup of coffee or, more likely, tea sat on the other side, looking like it hadn't been touched in some time. The office chair at the desk was empty, but Gregor sat in a wicker seat that faced the open back door, dressed informally in a short-sleeved shirt and a pair of cloth pants cinched with a drawstring. His sandals revealed a gnarled pair of feet that seemed even older than he was. The skin of his face looked gray and pasty, like Deidra could press her finger into his cheek and it would leave a finger-sized hole. He stared into the distance with an empty expression on his face.

"You already know why I'm here," she said.

"Yes," Gregor said. His voice sounded like old concrete. His eyes were bloodshot. "Matthew is dead."

Deidra pulled the desk chair over to Gregor's side, and sat down.

"I'm sorry," she said.

She imagined Papa sitting here where she was, which brought tears welling into her eyes. She blinked hard. No. There was too much on the line to let herself break down now. She hadn't cried earlier, she wasn't going to cry now.

"How is your arm?"

"It hurts, Dr. Iwal is working on it. Should have it healed over in a few days maybe."

"That's good."

They sat for several moments. Outside the door came the sounds of recovery—engines grinding, rubble being removed, voices calling in anger or surprise.

"They know where we are," Gregor said.

"Yes," Deidra said, understanding that *they* were the United Government.

"And they know we can't match their production."

"Maybe."

Gregor's gaze fell on her then. It was heavy and scalding. "You are young, Deidra. You will make many mistakes. This is all right. The people of Universe Three are familiar with problems and the mistakes that come from our kind of struggle. They will forgive them all as long as you keep one promise."

"Which is?"

"You have to promise you will never lie to yourself."

Deidra smirked, then moved the fingers of her bad arm so she could feel the dull ache that came through the pain retardant. Gregor may be an old man, and his advice may sometimes be as outdated as he was, but he was speaking the truth here.

"We have to leave Atropos City," she said.

Gregor nodded.

"You and Papa talked about it in the past. We have to find other planets, places where we can settle—more than one—places where we can grow without fear of attack."

Gregor sighed and blinked.

"That's the real reason you're here, isn't it?" he said. "You didn't come to tell me about Matthew. You came to ensure my support."

"I need you," Deidra said. "My father played the long game, and I know a lot of that is because of you. But I am truly sorry about Matt. We've both lost someone in this mess, now. I was coming here before the attack to give you the news."

"I'm tired," he said.

"I may not know much, but I figure it's going to get worse before it gets better."

He laughed. It was a thin laugh, but a laugh full of emotions, one she couldn't decipher fully.

"I need you to work with our planners to develop a plan. We have another Star Drive coming ready soon. We need to use it to shuttle people to as many places as makes sense. We need to ensure communications are available. There are plans to make, Gregor, and I need you to deal with them."

"What are you going to do?"

She was silent long enough that Gregor craned his head to look at her.

Deidra looked out over the rubble that the UG attack had created, and at the people who were working to recover. She thought of Jamal and the calm sense of balance he brought to her life, and she thought of Kel, beautiful Kel, both of them, buried in the remains of the house that she had considered her home until earlier today when the skimmers came and made everything a mess.

"I'm going to repair *Icarus*," she said. "And then I'm going to make the Uglies wish they had never come here."

NEWS

SOURCE: INFOWAVE — NEWS for the twenty-third century
DATE: February 20, 2215, Earth Standard
HEADLINE: Terrorists Strike Earth

London, New York, and Beijing were destroyed by devastating surprise attack today when Universe Three used their stolen Excelsior spacecraft to achieve Terran orbit for nearly two hours. The attack obliterated civilian and military personnel, damaged satellite communications, and destroyed several key manufacturing facilities that supported communities across the Solar System as well.

Casualties are unknown at this time, but are estimated to be upward of 100 million people either dead or injured.

SOURCE: INFOWAVE — NEWS for the twenty-third century
DATE: February 28, 2215, Earth Standard
HEADLINE: U3 Launches Multiple Attacks

*In the wake of Universe Three's cowardly attack on Earth last week, two
separate Universe Three attacks occurred in sequence today. The first
destroyed mining capability in the commercial sector of the asteroid belt, the
second disrupted manufacturing segments on Io. The damage was relatively
slight in relation to the attack on Earth, but the action, when paired with the
uptick in incidents of U3 terrorism across the Solar System, suggests that
Universe Three may have completed production of their second Star Drive
spacecraft, giving them numerical advantage.*

*"That won't last long," said Kevin LaPierre, the UG's new press secretary.
"Universe Three is pressing their luck now because they know we are just
months, if not weeks away from matching them."*

SOURCE: INFOWAVE — NEWS for the twenty-third century
DATE: July 30, 2215, Earth Standard
HEADLINE: Interstellar Command Gets Two New Ships

"We are excited today to reveal not one, but two new Excelsior class Star Drive spacecraft," *Press Secretary Kevin LaPierre said today. UGIS* Venture *and UGIS* Voyager *were commissioned and ran their maiden jumps.*

When teamed with Orion, *this gives the Solar System an advantage over the Universe Three terrorists who have been attacking with nearly free will.*

LaPierre added, "The three defensive ships will be stationed at critical locations to reduce U3's ability to hurt our citizens. Now that these are in place, the mighty production capability of the Solar System's people will be directed to build an attack fleet that will shut down this war once and forever."

SOURCE: INFOWAVE — NEWS for the twenty-third century
DATE: August 15, 2215, Earth Standard
HEADLINE: Surprise Attack Destroys Venus Station

A devastating attack on the science stations of Venus Station, a floating city in Venusian orbit, has resulted in thousands killed and a rescue operation of unprecedented scale.

"This should not have been able to happen," said Admiral Naomi Umaro. "The people of the Solar System will be revenged."

PROLOGUES

GALOPAR

Galopar
Local Date: Undefined
Local Time: Undefined

The landing had been hard—a half-crash, half-controlled tumble that ended with the Z-pad upside down and with a sliver of metal jabbed into his thigh. After extracting the metal and tending the wound, it took him an hour to get out of the skimmer. Another to rest up and gather what few items he could carry with him. A few blankets, a knife, and some energy bars. The emergency first aid kit.

He wished he had the painkiller back.

———

Nimchura limped across what had at one time been the perimeter of the UG's secret base camp, leaning hard on the branch he had cut from a tree to act as his crutch. He was just in time. The planet's sun was setting. It would be dark soon. Nimchura remembered the sound of this place's nocturnal predators. He didn't want to be out during the darkest, deepest part of the night. He had come too far to die that way.

His hand hurt as it gripped the rough bark. His leg throbbed and his back ached. Hunger gnawed at the pit of his stomach, and sweat drenched the cloth he had tied over his head to keep the insects off.

The walk to the camp took an entire day.

But he had found it.

The barracks were still up. The mess tent had been mostly reclaimed by the planet, but he found bins of vacuum-packed meals there, thank God, as his aunt would have said. He ripped the first open and gnawed on something that was supposed to be protein. "These things have a half-life of three universes," Deuce had once said to him. Which was still true—the meal was as disgusting as these things ever were, but that didn't matter now.

He ate until his stomach was comfortable.

There was enough here to keep him alive while he figured out how to deal with the land on his own.

In the distance, he saw the flat slabs of the landing pads that he and Alex Jarboe had poured so many years ago. They were cracked, but still there.

Other buildings were in the area, too.

Places where spaceships had been built.

Places where components still lay.

The sky grew darker as he leaned on the walking stick and headed to the barracks. He crossed an open area and recalled the last late-night conversation he held with Jarboe. He stopped then, and gazed up into the darkening indigo sky, watching as the first stars appeared.

Assuming his leg was up to it, and assuming he didn't get himself eaten by something overnight, tomorrow he would take inventory of the production line.

Tomorrow, if he could, he would begin building his own damned spacecraft.

It would be a beautiful thing, he thought.

He would call it an XB-25 Quadruple Firebrand.

Then Todias Nimchura, the only human being alive on the planet known as Galopar, turned and walked to the barracks.

He was alone.

Completely on his own.

For the first time in his life, he thought he might actually understand what freedom meant.

37 GEM

U3 Ship *Icarus*, 37 Geminorum System
Local Date: Undefined
Ship Time: 1245

A sense of loneliness settled over Deidra Francis as she sat at the head of the conference table and watched her advisers argue.

She missed her father, of course.

She missed her mother.

She missed having Kel and Jamal to buffer her from her anger. Even now, months after the UG had murdered them, it was hard to imagine a world without the two of them. She missed their touch, the heat of their bodies in the middle of the night, and simply the comforting weight their voices brought to discussions about philosophy, culture, or any one of a hundred different topics.

Deidra even missed her brat brothers, though both were useless in operational issues like this.

She thought about Katriana Martinez. At least they had a session planned later this evening when Katriana would guide *Vengeance* here to sync up the logistics of the three communities.

Assigning Katriana to command their second Star Drive spaceship had been the right call, even though it cost Deidra a confidante. Katriana was working with Deidra's mother and Gregor, helping the two of them direct the development of the other two new colonies that would be the backbone of Universe Three's future.

Papa should have scattered their resources earlier.

Looking back on it, Deidra could see that was the root of her father's primary mistake.

Focusing everything they had on Atropos City at one time had, admittedly, resulted in getting them a second Star Drive craft in only a few years, but it had also given the Uglies the ability to wipe them out in one barrage.

That wouldn't happen again, Deidra thought as she rubbed the headache from her temple. At least not as long as she was in control of the organization.

She had been firm.

Three settlements, scattered about the stars.

Three places to hide. Three places to grow.

Universe Three would expand from there, but it would expand slowly, and in a way that made sense.

And what made sense to Deidra was that, while each colony would be designed to be able to subsist on its own in case of emergency, the colony here in the 37 Gem system would be responsible for one thing, and one thing only: build spaceships.

Their Scorpii colony would focus on education, training, and the scientific research required to stay ahead of the UG. The group that populated the Capella double system would be responsible for agricultural support and expanding the food stock of all their populations.

Deidra cleared her throat, but the argument was going strong enough that only a few noticed her.

That made her happy.

They had been going at it for thirty minutes, which suggested that they weren't yet fully united, despite the raids they had already successfully executed. This was fine by her. Though she no longer agreed with her father's fundamental idea of their enemy, Papa had taught her the value of open discussion within her team. Difference of opinion was good. Conflict held value.

To a point.

"37 Gem has four planets with the base ability to support life," said Kyleen Lian, who had taken control of the organization's entire bio-agriculture program and run it well. In only a few months, she and her staff had designed a system that should support all three of their outposts.

Kazima Yamada replied. "Yes," she said. "But we are thin now. We have only three thousand people to create this station. So we need to focus on one only."

Deidra cleared her throat again, this time loud enough to bring the rest to a halt. She rubbed her arm where it still ached despite having healed.

"Kazima is right," she said. "Focus, remember. The question at hand is not how many settlements we will have here at first, the question for 37 Gem is only how quickly can it build another Star Drive."

"But the other planets—" Lian said.

"Once the base colony is designed, we can charter operations to use the other planets for lifeboats in case of attack," Deidra said. "And if we are here long enough, we'll consider permanent expansion. But one step at a time."

The group settled.

Refocused, it began to make headway.

Deidra sat back, once again feeling the shell of loneliness collapse over her.

———

It was important to Deidra that they met in the common mess, so that's where she took her seat—a booth up on the raised platform, far enough away from others to allow for private conversation, but visible enough to make a presence. It was something her father would have done, something that broke barriers between her and the people of Universe Three. They were at war now. Full and open war. It was important the people feel like she was one of them. She had been excited to see Katriana again, so she was already seated when her mentor arrived.

"It's good to see you again," Katriana said as she settled into the seat across the table from Deidra.

"You, too," she replied.

Katriana's tray carried a curry dish, and a warm tea that steamed when she took the lid off its container. Deidra was having a grilled burger that had seemed like a better idea when she picked it out than it did now, a piece of bio-base banana, and what was probably too big of a slice of cake.

"Your mother asked me if you are eating right."

"And you told her?"

Katriana took in the cake and shrugged.

"How is life on *Vengeance*?" Deidra said, smiling. It felt good to have a friend here.

"More busy than I imagined."

"Glad to hear it."

They both ate for a moment.

Katriana was nearly two decades older than Deidra, and she looked about as tired as Deidra felt. The pace of their movements and the decisions had been daunting.

"How are you feeling?" Katriana said.

"We've got a lot to do, but I think the team came up with a good plan today. We should have a real ground presence in two weeks. Base manufacturing up and running in six months. Maybe another Star Drive a year later," she said, smiling. "Assuming UG doesn't suss us out before then."

She didn't have to say that *Icarus* and *Vengeance* would spend a good chunk of that time running guerilla operations in the Solar System in order to keep UG off balance enough to give 37 Gem cover.

"That's not what I asked."

Deidra frowned.

Katriana put her fork down, reached across the table, and placed her hand over Deidra's. "I asked how you are feeling."

"Fine," Deidra said.

Her friend nodded, then withdrew her hand, leaving a chilled spot at the back of Deidra's.

"I was barely older than you when I lost my girls," Katriana said.

"Rosa and Talia. I know how hard it makes you. You lose people, and you dry up like cane."

"You were strong enough for them, though," Deidra said.

"No."

"You made it through."

"I guess. But those are two different things."

"How did you do that?" Until she said it, Deidra hadn't realized this was the question that she had been wanting to ask Katriana since the day the UG ripped up Atropos City.

"How did you keep your sanity?" she added.

Katriana shook her head absently. "I thought of them every day."

"I'm doing that now, and it's killing me."

Katriana took a sip of her hot tea and grimaced as she swallowed it down. The lines that ran down her cheeks grew stronger as her expression tightened.

"I know. Every time I thought about my girls I felt like someone took a razor and slashed my heart. The world felt so big and terrible. I wanted to curl up and die. I wanted to quit because there was nothing I could do. But, every time I thought about that I realized that doing that meant that my girls wouldn't have mattered."

"So you decided to strike back."

"I decided to make whatever difference I could, regardless of how little that might be."

Deidra looked around the room.

Perhaps forty people were here, eating, talking with friends. None of them could do this alone, and yet together they formed a group that was preparing to make Star Drive spacecraft on a planet that had never before even had a human visitor. An image of Ellyn Parker climbing the human pyramid came over her, the sound of Papa's voice reverberating in her memory. She thought of Matt Anderson and Timmon Keyes leaving the briefing room together after a pre-mission brief.

She raised her fork and took a bite of cake.

It was sugary and chocolate.

"Thank you," she said after she swallowed it down. "Can I ask you another question?"

"Of course."

"Are you proud of yourself?"

Katriana gazed away and a distant smile came to her lips. Then the smile grew warm and her gaze returned to Deidra's, her brown eyes showing a hint of moisture at their corners.

"I don't know," she said. "But I still think of my girls every day. I hope they know I love them."

"I'm proud of you," Deidra said.

Katriana smiled, and glanced at their plates. "Thank you," she said. "Now eat your dinner or I'll have to tell your mother I've lied to her."

"We wouldn't want that, now, would we?"

"No," Katriana said. "We wouldn't want that."

EUROPA

Europa Station
Local Date: Classified
Local Time: Classified

Torrance stood at the edge of Europa Station's observation deck, which was a little compartment that was currently positioned to stare out at Jupiter. The radiation-hardened coating of the shield was older technology, giving the orange striations that ran through the gas giant a green tint. He had just come from Marisa's compartment. She was doing well—the burns had healed, and the DNA therapy was doing its best to rebuild her skin. Torrance figured she was nearly out of the woods now because she was joking with him one moment and calling him out on his bullshit the next.

That made him happy.

Or, if not exactly happy, at least content in a way that felt right. The future was, of course, uncertain, but now he felt confident that she would be part of it.

As he stood on the observation deck, however, Torrance was not thinking about Marisa.

Instead, he was thinking about the cloud cover that encased the planet, a hydrogen and helium atmosphere that surrounded the planet's metallic core in a configuration and composition that made Jupiter almost more of a sun than a planet. By mass, it was nearly three times the size of the rest of the Solar System's planets, combined. A little more oomph, Torrance thought, and perhaps it would have collapsed to form a star itself.

His morning brief said that a college class was coming tomorrow to run an exercise that would have them launch an instrumentation probe into the planet's atmosphere so they could learn about orbital dynamics and chaotic weather patterns.

Torrance smiled at that.

It wasn't that long ago that he was standing on a different observation deck and contemplating the effects of another exercise designed to put probes into a different ball of hydrogen and helium.

Had he made a good decision then?

How would everything be different if he hadn't completed that mission? Probably not much. There's always another guy, anyway. Always someone who will do the job.

Still.

A hundred million people dead in two hours.

Jesus.

Even months later, the size of that destruction was staggering.

He shook his head. What can one man do in this world? What can you do when events are so big and the wheels of power and fate turn in ways no one can expect?

Torrance had taken his position as the UG ambassador to Europa a month before *Venture* and *Voyager* were launched. It was a strange place to be—full of academics and mega-brains that weren't afraid to have opinions about politics and the military. A place where the hallways were full of arguments.

His office was a corner nook of the Excelsior wing of the Jovian Science Center, which was the consortium responsible for the design, assembly, test, and staffing of what was planned to be the UGIS *Magellan*, the first, and possibly only spacecraft that the United Government would build for nonmilitary purposes.

He was a bit of an enigma in the center, part war hero, part government crony, part technical guru.

In other words, every day was full of stress.

"It's beautiful, isn't it?" Jared Kulpani asked as he stepped to Torrance's side. Kulpani, Torrance's new boss, was JSC's president and he looked the part—tall and athletic enough that it was clear Kulpani was a runner or biker or regular participant in some other sport. Torrance made a mental note to find out what that was. As president, Kulpani was the ranking civilian officer on Europa Station, and as ranking civilian officer he held sway over most every decision he wanted to hold sway of.

"Yes, it's beautiful."

"How is Lieutenant Harthing?"

"Better every day."

"That's good. Settled in to your quarters, yet?"

"Yes. Maybe. I guess." Torrance hesitated, feeling that awkward sense he got when it came to chitchat. "I can't say that anything's really felt like home since *Everguard*, to be perfectly honest."

"I suppose it takes time."

"That's true enough." Torrance gripped the rail before him. "It's fun to be around so many smart people, though. That's the thing I liked best about being a systems leader. It's good to be somewhere I can at least pretend to be technical."

"We do have a bucketload of brains here, that's for sure."

Torrance managed to succeed in his efforts not to roll his eyes. The term *bucketload of brains* was distinctly hated by every member of the staff as far as he could tell, so Kulpani's use of it let Torrance know how far out of touch the president was.

Not that it mattered.

"How can I help you," Torrance said, getting his mind fully back into gear in his role as ambassador.

"I had an application come across my desk this morning that I thought you might be interested in."

"Really?"

Torrance wondered if Reyes had briefed the president during his visit a month prior. It would be like Reyes to plant such triggers with a leader like Kulpani.

"Does the name Thomas Kitchell ring a bell?"

Torrance couldn't help but smile. "It does at that," he said. "Do tell on."

"He wants to come here for an internship next semester."

"I would give him the highest recommendation, sir," Torrance said. "It would be great to see him."

"I'm glad to hear it, especially since his application specifies that he wants to work under you."

"Is that so?" Torrance said.

"He's been quite explicit. He comes to work under you, on a special project of your choosing, or he's going accept a role with the Mars observatory system. His scores are already at the top of his class, and I understand he's quite persuasive—so I can see why he's interested in the ambassadorial side of the fence. I know this is technically outside his academic program, but I would hate to lose him."

"I concur with that."

"Should I tell him we accept his conditions?"

Torrance grinned and glanced back out at the clouds of Jupiter. He put his hands in his pockets, and felt his right hand close around the hard surface of the data crystal that still held the Eden data.

With everything going on, he hadn't been able to bring himself to look at it.

He had planned to, of course.

He wanted to.

But he couldn't tell himself that it mattered anymore, and to be fully truthful with himself, he wasn't sure he could handle the idea of study after study ending in failure. So the idea of doing more work on the cube had left an ugly taste in his mouth. Even if he found something, he wasn't sure that bringing an alien race into the mix of human politics today was particularly smart.

But Thomas Kitchell wanted to work with him.

The news was like a light switch hitting his adrenaline spigot.

A sense of optimism welled up in him stronger than any he had felt since…well…since he was on *Everguard*.

"Do you ever get the idea that the most important things we do in our lives don't really have much to do with our jobs?" Torrance said.

"I suppose that depends on your job," Kulpani said.

"Maybe you're right," Torrance replied.

But that was a lie as far as he was concerned. Thomas Kitchell was coming to work for him, and he was coming to work on a project that was outside Kitchell's formal program of study, and a project no one else would understand.

Not yet, anyway.

Maybe never.

But Kitchell was coming, and despite everything else that was happening across the universe, that made Torrance happy. It made him feel like there was some kind of hope still left.

Still, he lied and said the president was right.

So maybe Reyes had been right when he told Torrance that he had the skills to do this job.

"So, do we accept Thomas Kitchell?" Kulpani said.

"Yeah," Torrance replied. "But when you do, I want you to tell him he'll have to toe a tight line here. Tell him that as long as he does that, I'm pretty much always willing to take a chance."

"Great," Kulpani said. "I'll do that." He turned to walk away.

"I mean it," Torrance said, grabbing the president's arm. "Word for word, all right?"

Kulpani seemed uncertain, but said, "Sure."

Then he left Torrance alone to stare out into the clouds surrounding Jupiter, which he did for the next hour until Europa Station rotated such that the view was filled with the velvety darkness of deep space, highlighted by a pattern of stars.

NEWS

SOURCE: INFOWAVE — NEWS for the twenty-third century
DATE: August 20, 2215, Earth Standard
HEADLINE: Retaliation Finds Empty Nest

"They aren't there," said Press Secretary Kevin LaPierre as he displayed photographic evidence of a desolate Atropos City, the place that until just recently was known to be the home base for the renegade terrorist organization Universe Three.

It was clear that the civilization was evacuated recently, leaving even some construction in semi-completion in order to abandon the city. The photos revealed a ghost town that was at times unnerving in its simplicity. The stories they revealed spoke of the difficult lives that were likely led there.

"This is good news and bad news," LaPierre added at one point. "It means that Interstellar Command has the upper hand, but it also means that Deidra Francis and the rest of the U3 leadership structure has likely split itself."

LaPierre avoided several direct questions, but the prevailing wisdom seems to be that this interstellar war has now entered a new and very difficult phase.

"We're not sure how to win a guerilla war in space," one adviser said off the record. "This could get very ugly."

THANK YOU!
THIS IS THE END OF STARCLASH

If you enjoyed this story, please consider stopping by your favorite
online booksellers' websites to leave a review.

Word of mouth is the most powerful force in the universe when it
comes to the livelihood of your favorite authors. Even a few words can
help!

THE STORY CONTINUES!
AN ARMS RACE ACROSS THE GALAXY

Reeling from war, the United Government's Interstellar Command wants control. In constant fear of discovery, Universe Three wants revenge. Amid a changing starscape of intrigue Torrance Black—hero turned science ambassador—gets one more chance to find intelligent life outside the Solar System: convince the most prominent scientists alive to spend one of their precious Star Drive missions on a trip to Alpha Centauri A.

Win and he saves an alien species. Lose and his career is done. How far is Torrance willing to go?

How far will he have to go?

STARBOUND, the fifth book of of *Stealing the Sun,* a space based Science Fiction series from bestselling science fiction and dark fantasy author Ron Collins.

READER LIST SIGN-UP

Get copies of STARCRUISE (a stand-alone short story in the STEALING THE SUN SERIES), and Glamour of the God-Touched, volume 1 of Saga of the God-Touched Mage for Free!

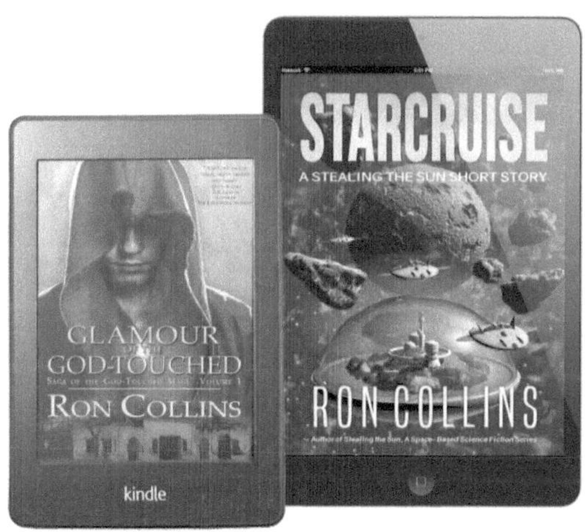

Sign-up at: https://www.typosphere.com/newsletter

ALSO BY RON COLLINS

Novels

Stealing the Sun (9 books)

Saga of the God-Touched Mage (8 books)

The PEBA Diaries (2 books)

The Knight Deception

Wakers

Poetry

Five Seven Five

(Science fictional examinations of the elusive haiku)

Collections

Collins Creek (Three Volumes)

Tomorrow in All the Worlds

Picasso's Cat & Other Stories

Five Magics

Seven Days in May (with John C. Bodin)

Nonfiction

On Writing (And Reading!) Short

(A Science Fiction Writer's Quest for Stories that Matter)

ABOUT RON COLLINS

Ron Collins is a best-selling Science Fiction and Dark Fantasy author who writes across the spectrum of speculative fiction.

His short fiction has received a Writers of the Future prize and a CompuServe HOMer Award. His short story "The White Game" was nominated for the Short Mystery Fiction Society's Derringer Award. With his daughter, Brigid Collins, he edited the anthology *Face the Strange.*

He has contributed a couple hundred or so short stories to professional publications such as *Analog, Asimov's,* and several other magazines and anthologies (including several editions of the Fiction River Anthology Series). His latest science fiction series, *Stealing the Sun,* and his fantasy series *Saga of the God-Touched Mage* are available from Skyfox publishing.

He holds a degree in Mechanical Engineering, and has worked to develop avionics systems, electronics, and information technology before chucking it all to write full-time.

facebook.com/roncollinssfwriter

twitter.com/roncollins13

instagram.com/roncollinssfwriter

bookbub.com/authors/ron-collins

goodreads.com/Ron_Collins

amazon.com/Ron-Collins/e/B00AP2IYEW

ACKNOWLEDGMENTS

As always, I would like to thank John Bodin and Sharon Bass for their outstanding work and diligence in helping me with early drafts. Their effort is greatly appreciated.

I also want to thank Mike Resnick for his support throughout my career as well as for taking the time to give me such a fantastic endorsement. Very little is more thrilling than to have a writer like Mike say such nice things.

And finally, I want to thank my wife and copyeditor extraordinaire Lisa Collins for her usual fantastic work, and for going above and beyond the call by providing insights that were critical to making this work what it is. As always, all errors are mine!